KoKo

A NOVEL

BIEN-AIMÈ WENDA

No part of this book may be reproduced or transmitted in any form or by any means, electronic or mechanical, including photocopying, recording or by any information storage and retrieval system, without written permission from the author.

This is a work of fiction. Names, characters, businesses, places, events and incidents are either the products of the author's imagination or used in a fictitious manner. Any resemblance to actual persons, living or dead, or actual events is purely coincidental.

Copyright © 2018 Bien-Aimé Wenda
All rights reserved.
Cover design by Blazing Covers
ISBN-13: 978-0692079669 (Bien-Aime Indie Books)
ISBN-10: 0692079661

KOKO

For

the

bookworms

CHAPTER ONE

Koreen Wilson

Make no mistake about it: I absolutely love my fiancé. He is my rock, my biggest supporter, and my best friend. He's the best father to our only child, J'adore. I'm his queen and he's my king. I love him to pieces; from the ends of the earth and back. There's no one else I would prefer to spend the rest of my life with. Despite of all this mushy shit, our sex life is trash and for that reason, I have been living a double life as a habitual cheater. A bisexual nympho.

Before you hypocrites start coming for me and accuse me of not appreciating the good man that I have, why don't y'all put yourselves in my red bottoms? When Pierre and I first met, he knew that I wasn't just Koreen Wilson. I was *Koreen The Dream Wilson*. I was *the* video vixen and just about every man and woman's fantasy. Not to mention a pioneer in the hip hop modeling industry.

Despite being the opposite hue of most of the "it" girls in the business, my flawless ebony skin, sharp cheekbones, confident white smile, and innocent brown eyes made me the most sought after and highest paid video vixen in the game. I can brag that I single-handedly brought dark-skinned women back as the most desired women in the game. Before then, us dark-chocolate girls had barriers to overcome in the entertainment industry and I helped bust that shit wide open. I held my head up high and strutted with the poise and self-assurance of the Queen of Sheba everywhere I went. I was the shit and I made sure everyone knew it. Not only was I a natural beauty, but my work ethic and ambition made me a force to be reckoned with, helping me to land the cover of every major black magazine spread, as well as the lead girl in every hot hip hop artists' music video.

    Before meeting Pierre, I was married to hip hop artist, Bernard *'Lyrical Bernz'* Ingram, for five years. I met Bernie my freshman year at Miami Northwestern High. From the moment Bernard laid eyes on me, he was infatuated. He made it known from jump that he wanted me, often telling me that I was sexy and beautiful *"for a dark-skinned girl"*, as if that were a compliment. It was strange to me because before then, I never considered myself that attractive but unlike the other brown girls I knew, the thought of bleaching never crossed my mind. I noticed early on that it was always the "lite-brites" (my term for anyone lighter than me) that admired my dark mahogany complexion and it was usually the ones as dark or darker than me, who tried to put me down for being dark. It was nothing but self-hate, honey. Anyway, long story short, me and Bernard became high school sweethearts and unbeknownst to him, he helped me to become comfortable in my own skin.

    Back then, Bernie had dreams of becoming a rap star and I had aspirations of being an actress. I participated in every school play and was the proud member of the glee and drama club each year. Bernie only participated in talent shows and couldn't be bothered with school clubs. He was either always in the studio recording mix tapes or trying to get his music to the local radio stations. By the time we had both graduated from Northwestern High, Bernie had gained a little underground fame. We both knew he was at the brink of success when a record exec requested to meet with him. When Bernard flew to New York to meet with the executives at MorningStarr Recordz, he was offered a contract and an advance of one hundred thousand dollars, which he eagerly accepted. With his debut single, *Lemme Put it on You*, taking the country by storm, Bernie, aka "Lyrical Bernz", became an overnight sensation. Luckily for me, Bernard was able to pull some strings and I was given the chance to play his love interest in his *Lemme Put it on You* music video. It would be my first video shoot ever and the beginning of my journey as video vixen, *Koreen the Dream*.

Bernie and I had a courthouse wedding soon after the success of *Lemme Put it on You*. Although I still had dreams of becoming an actress, my modeling career had begun to take off during our first year of marriage. I had become the most recognized video vixen in the hip hop industry. Unfortunately for him, Bernie would become a one-hit wonder and his label soon dropped him after his second album, *Bern with Me* flopped. I always suspected that his resentment towards my success had led to the depression and infidelity that followed. Flying out of Miami to different locations regularly, made it that much easier for Bernard to indulge in a string of extramarital affairs.

It was during the last year of my marriage that offers for movie roles in urban films finally began pouring in but I had to decline. Bernie and I found out we would be parents for the first time and decided it would be best for me to take a year off from working. We did however, agree to a reality show, *Koreen Unfiltered,* on a popular up-and-coming urban network. Unfortunately for me, I hadn't anticipated the loss of our still-born baby girl, Ayanna, being filmed on national television.

As if leaving the hospital without our baby wasn't devastating enough, my marriage was turning to shit and was being exposed right in-front of viewers. Week after week, viewers, gossip shows, and bloggers criticized and judged our marriage. True enough, I had agreed to a reality show, but I didn't think it was anyone's business as to why I chose to stay by my man's side; and that was just what I told our fans and our haters on social media platforms. When Bernie and I had finally stopped sleeping in the same bedroom, I could not bring myself to leave him. I loved that man and was loyal to him. He was the only guy I had ever been with. He had known me and been there for me long before I had become *Koreen the Dream*. It was because of Bernard that I had had my big break. Yeah, he often cheated, but I still felt that he genuinely loved me for me and not my money, my body, or my fame. I was hopeful that he would one day snap out of his depression and become the supportive man I once knew.

Although my parents pleaded with me to leave Bernie from the very beginning, it took me five years to end my marriage. What finally broke the camel's back was coming home unexpectedly and finding Bernard with a look of complete bliss on his face, as he anal-fucked my trifling-ass cousin, Gary, on our bed. If that wasn't bad enough, the camera crew from our reality show had come in with me and caught my surprise on film. That episode alone had made reality show history being the highest-rated TV program that night, as 3.2 million viewers witnessed my humiliation. That had been enough for me. It was hands down, one of the most gut-wrenching and difficult experiences I had ever had to go through. With all of the temptations I had run into during the early years of my career, not once had I ever contemplated cheating on Bernard, *ever*.

    I refused to shoot any more seasons of *Koreen Unfiltered* after divorcing Bernie, resulting in a long legal battle with the network. My marriage, the loss of my daughter, my lack of privacy, and the insensitive judgements from the media left me jaded. Some days, I refused to get out of bed and would sink into a deep depression. Food quickly became my comfort, leading to an addiction of binge eating, and before I knew it, I was weighing close to 260 pounds. I let myself pack on so much weight, that the agency that represented me, was forced to drop me as a client. I stayed away from blogs and deactivated my social media accounts after countless and cruel memes mocking my shocking weight gain, went viral. I stopped watching one of my favorite late night talk shows after hearing Ms. Mindy Mathers, the Queen of Mean, gossip about how fat I'd gotten.

Even with Bernie out of my life, I still managed to become a running trend week after week.

A year after my divorce, I was contacted by a reality T.V. show, offering a substantial amount of money to join their celebrity weight loss edition. I declined the offer and opted to hire a celebrity fitness trainer instead. I went through an agency and per my request to send the best of the best, the agency sent out my current fiancé, Pierre Woods, to train me. I was immediately impressed. Pierre was 6'2 with nice bright teeth, nice hard abs, a sexy cleft on his milk chocolate chin, and sported neat sexy shoulder-length locs. He was and still is the most patient and respectful man I had ever come across. Most of all, he was extremely humble; a trait I had become unaccustomed to since becoming a celebrity. Long story short, the attraction was mutual and before I knew it, Pierre and I were hitting the sack regularly, which I will admit, helped in shedding 130 pounds.

Thanks to Pierre, I was looking better than ever and had made a successful come-back within a year. This time, I was determined to revamp my image as a fat, divorced, former vixen and ex-wife of a gay rapper. I no longer wanted to be known as *Koreen the Dream*. I re-introduce myself to the entertainment industry as *KoKo*, which had always been Pierre's nickname for me.

Now that I was single, and only had my income to depend on, I was even more driven and focused on adding to my net worth. The sensitive and naïve Koreen was long gone. After being with only Bernie since high school, I was ready to date, have fun and go buck wild. I wasn't looking to weigh myself down with another relationship. I had just turned twenty-four that June and wanted to do things other twenty-four-year-olds were doing. I didn't want to invest myself in another relationship, just to have my spirit broken again. Besides, with multiple bookings, club appearances, and flights all over the world, I didn't have time for a serious relationship and I reminded Pierre of that repeatedly. He was also reminded that I had just gotten out of a 5-year marriage and he insisted that he was crystal clear of what our relationship was: *friends with benefits.*

Even after confiding in Pierre about my sexcapades with the rich and famous in explicit details, Pierre still chose to be *"faithful"* to me. He seemed to only have eyes for me, but I wasn't surprised. Many men were mesmerized by my attitude, hour-glass shape, and dark-chocolate skin. But if you asked him, he'd swear it had nothing to do with the physical. He said it was my aura, confidence, and genuine personality that he loved about me. I never believed him. Either way, he fell in love with me and pursued me with a greater vengeance, but he just wasn't my type. There were only two type of men I would even consider seriously dating at that time: wealthy hip hop artists or anyone else in the industry who could help me advance further in my career. Pierre was neither. He was wealthy but that was about it. He was also cultured, vegan, self-educated, and heavily into holistic medicine.

After wearing me down for another year, I finally relented and gave Pierre Woods a chance. Since then, he has been and is the yin to my yang. My parents love him almost as much as I do. He's definitely everything I never knew I was missing in my life.........minus our boring-ass sex life.

CHAPTER TWO
KoKo

I've hidden my sexual appetite for women from Pierre throughout our entire relationship, but I had good reason to. He was way too reserved and adamantly opposed homosexuality. He was brought up in a family of bourgeois Catholics. If he knew just how much of a freak I really was, and the details of my current sexcapades, there is no doubt that Pierre would break off our engagement. Now that I was a mother to our 2-year-old little girl, J'adore *(whom we affectionately nicknamed Jada)*, there was no way I was going to let Pierre find out. I was determined for our daughter to be raised in a 2-parent home like we both had been.

Call me whatever you want, I don't care. I had an overactive sex-drive and I needed variety. I got tired of Pierre's routine missionary position whenever we made love. He never wanted to try new things in the bedroom. I was growing tired of trying to convince Pierre that it didn't make me a 'whore' if I asked him to pull my hair, spank my ass, or unload his semen in my mouth. He always rejected my ideas claiming I was "too much of a queen" in his eyes. We were now both only 27, with the sex life of a bunch of sixty-year-olds. Hell, there were probably sixty-year-olds getting more spontaneity from their man than I was. Nevertheless, this is the reason why I had standing freak sessions with music video director by the name of Biggz, Ganja Green, a popular reggae artist, and the very sexy but very married, Moet. All on different days, of course.

    Today was Biggz's day. I had met him about a year ago at Fort Lauderdale beach on the set of a video shoot I was doing for R&B bad boy, Tristan Greene. The song was featuring rapper, Brick Boss, and the set was filled with the rapper's sketchy looking entourage. I later found out that Biggz was related to the rapper and that was believable because the resemblance was uncanny. Not only was he just as fat as Brick Boss, but his cocoa-colored skin was also hidden underneath his collection of tatts and his manicured facial hair. Even his bald head was covered completely in tatted quotes and poems like Brick's. Decked out in designer shorts, they were all dressed for the beach. Some followed Brick's lead and walked around the set shirtless. Biggz and a few others spared us the sight of sagging male boobs and paraded around with heavy gold chains on top of white tank tops.

    I was getting prepped by the makeup crew behind the camera man wearing nothing but 6-inch gold stilettos and a shiny gold Versace string bikini that barely covered my areola. My head felt heavy with the weight of an oversized Foxy-Brown-type afro wig sewn on top of my braids. Between the makeup crew struggling with the heat, and my heels annoying me by continually sinking into the searing golden sand, I was highly irritable and ready to just make this money and leave. I had been on the set since 4 a.m. and it was a little after 1 p.m. when the director's assistant finally shouted that he needed me to be oiled up and ready in 2 minutes.

Biggz, who unbeknownst to me, had been staring at me from across the set, bolted towards me as fast as his large frame allowed.

"I got that." Biggz said, snatching the bottle of coconut oil from the interning production assistant. The young college boy immediately looked at me, unsure of what was going on. I gave him a phony reassuring smile. "It's fine. Can you get me another bottle of water? Make sure its alkaline this time, please."

As the P.A. trotted off, Biggz immediately got to work. Squirting oil on his big calloused hands, he crouched down and started on my already-glistening long dark legs. He seemed to be in full concentration mode as he took his time rubbing my protruding ass with deep slow motions.

"You're Brick Boss' cousin, right?" I asked, wanting to be sure before he went any further.

"Yep, that's my cuzzo. I direct a lot of his videos." He answered from behind me as he made his way up the back of my thighs.

"Oh?" Interest piqued, he was suddenly a lot more attractive to me. "You only direct his videos?"

"Nah, I have a long list of artists whose videos I've directed. You ain't ever heard of me or my production company? Bigg Boyz Productions?" He asked, looking up at me.

I shook my head as he laughed. It was at that moment that I decided that I would use this to my advantage. Although I was already the most successful video vixen in the industry, I had to make sure I remained on top, *by all means.*

When we were done shooting for the day, I impatiently kicked off my stilettos and slid my feet in some comfortable sandals. After 12 hours and multiple wardrobe changes in the unrelenting heat, my manicured feet were not only covered in blisters, they were also barking. I couldn't wait to get home to my shower and let cool water travel down every crack and crevice of my fatigued athletic body.

I was surprise to see a smiling Biggz walking towards me. I had assumed that he had already left with Brick Boss and his entourage.

"What you smilin' for?" I asked.

He eyed my body up and down hungrily. "Somebody wasn't lying when they said the blacker the berry, the sweeter the juice." He flirted.

"You wouldn't know how sweet my juice is." I shot back.

"Wouldn't mind finding out." He smiled again. *"What are you doing?"* I shrieked as he picked me up in his muscular arms in one swoop.

He carried me across the sand towards the parking area. I was too exhausted to put up a fight and instead laid my head against his chest. I even ignored the scratches from his curled-up hairs, peeking from under his white tank top that felt like Brillo pads against me.

"Which one's yours?" He asked, glancing around the parking lot.

I pointed towards my Range Rover. "The white Rover."

KOKO

We reached my Rover and he placed me gently on my size seven feet. "I wanted to properly introduce myself and I didn't know when I would get another chance to see you again." He explained. "I'm Biggz. I wanna take you out sometime."

"Oh really?" I chuckled, amused. "Biggz? Is that what the ladies call you?"

His eyes lit up as he once again showcased his broad smile. "That's what everyone calls me. My government name's Malik."

"Nice to meet you Malik, I'm KoKo. Government name is Koreen."

"I know. Nice to meet you." He said, extending his hand. I politely shook it.

He couldn't stop smiling and I had to admit, he was kinda cute, even if he was a bit on the hefty side.

"So, you gonna let me take you out?" He asked sounding anxious.

"Well, I'm spoken for. I hope I didn't lead you on. I had no idea you were out here waitin' on me." I explained.

"It's alright. Your man's slackin', tho." He stated matter-of-factly, scanning the parking lot. "I don't see him picking you up from a long day of being on your feet. I don't even see you out here with bodyguards."

I laughed. "Bodygaurds? I ain't *that* famous."

"Psshhh, every-fuckin- body knows *Koreen the Dream-*"

"*KoKo.*" I cringed, quickly correcting him. I had come to hate my former stage name. I associated it with all of the hurt and humiliation of my past.

"My fault. *KoKo*." He apologized. "Look, I know you gotta man and all, but I still wanna get to know you. How about I leave you with my number and if you ever need anything, and I do mean *anything*, hit me up."

"Anything?" I teased, as he pulled a glossy gray business card from his pocket.

"*Anything*, baby girl." He repeated sincerely, gazing intensely into my dark brown eyes.

KOKO

CHAPTER THREE
Ivonka Roux

"You have a good man by your side who worships the ground you walk on and you're over here treating him like caca, *dios mio*. If you don't want him, *please* let me have him. Shit, let's swap husbands for a week." Desiree teased KoKo.

I didn't think it was a wise idea. It wasn't a secret that KoKo was territorial about her man. Not to mention a hot-head. I suspected her attitude and defensive nature stemmed from her rough upbringing in Miami.

"Look bitch, don't fuck with me. Pregnant or not, you will get fucked up. Ain't nobody touchin' my man but *me*." She threatened between puffs of her Newport. She threw a wink and smirk towards Desiree to let her know they were still cool but not to push it.

Des or Desi, as we preferred to call her, was always-pregnant, which meant she was always-emotional. At twenty-four, she was the baby of our trio and we treated her as such. Half Bahamian and half Cuban, Des was a biracial amazon towering at 5 feet 11. She had a head full of long fiery-red curls, a baby face, and was sometimes a little shy and soft spoken. She was highly intelligent but lacked common sense. She had been studying to become a registered nurse at the local community college on and off for the past 6 years and could have finished her nursing degree by now, if her husband wasn't always knocking her up.

"Really? Must you use that language in public?" I gave Koreen a stern look before glancing around *Trendies*, the dimly lit but crowded Caribbean café.

Trendies or *Trendy West Indie's Café & Lounge*, was located at the heart of South Beach and was often frequented by celebrities and tourists. For the past year, the girls and I tried to make it a weekly routine to catch up at Trendies. It was one of the few spots where the paparazzi were prohibited from loitering.

KoKo shrugged indifferently.

I eyed KoKo's stinky cigarette. One of her other bad habits that her fiancé, Pierre, knew nothing about. "And would you *please* put that cancer-stick out? Des is pregnant." I chastised in a hushed whisper.

"When isn't she pregnant?" She chortled, and Desiree gasped.

"You're such a bitch sometimes." Des stated with mock hurt, looking directly at KoKo.

"I'm very much aware, thank you. Y'all still love me though." She winked, then put out her cigarette.

Of the three of us, I considered myself the voice of reason. When KoKo and I first met, I had never heard of *Koreen the Dream* but knew she had to be famous when she hired me a few years ago to look over a contract of a reality show she was starring in. She had a 3-year contract with a major network and was desperate to find any loopholes in her obligations. The morning she came in my office to meet with me, I caught my employees ogling the vixen. I thought nothing of it because Koreen was and still is breathtakingly gorgeous, even without all of the artificial stuff she wore. You know what I'm talking about: the Malaysian hair, thick false lashes, and even the layers of makeup. She had natural beauty and an alluring hour glass figure. Not to mention, her rich dark hue and high fashion sense always caught the attention of others. Anyway, after successfully getting the network to settle, KoKo and I remained in contact. She's definitely one of the most blunt but down-to-earth celebrities I've encountered in the industry.

 I guess I should introduce myself. My name is Ivonka Nicolette Roux, one of the finest high-profile entertainment lawyer money could buy. My friends and family call my Vonne or Ivonne for short. Originally from Baton Rouge, Louisiana, I moved to South Florida after the death of my boss at a former firm I worked for. His inexperienced, misogynist, and obnoxious son soon took over his company and I decided that was my sign to leave and open my own practice. Looking to start fresh somewhere new and far from my old repetitive life, Miami seemed like the ideal place to relocate to for a jolt in my social life. Besides, what did I have to lose? I was single with no children. My deceased father and his siblings had migrated to Miami from Haiti, so it wasn't like I didn't have relatives to lean on in Florida.

 Other than KoKo and Des, I had no real friends down here. I met Desiree through KoKo not long after meeting Koreen. Des had shot a couple of video shoots with her before she had gotten married.

After having been here for about 4 years, I have no regrets about moving. I love the culture, nightlife, the people and especially the Caribbean cuisine. It gave me a chance to reconnect with my Haitian roots. Having been born with what some would call Creole features and my Baton Rouge accent, I sometimes stood out from the natives. I liked that my high yellow complexion stayed nicely tanned throughout the year, enhancing the look of my heart-shaped face, full round cheeks, and slightly slanted emerald-colored eyes. Although I had what some would controversially refer to as, '*good hair*', I kept my mane in a professional sleek shoulder-length bob at all times. Other than that, I had a slender 5-foot-7 frame with an ass I had purchased a few weeks ago from a surgeon KoKo had referred me to.

"Mmm, that ass looking right." Koreen said, eyeing my bulging ass in my Oscar De La Renta grey fitted slacks. "Told y'all that Dr. Jacobson is the shit. Look at that ass. Got me lookin' at you in a whole different way." She said before flicking her tongue at me.

"Look chick, for the umpteenth time, I am strictly dickly, you hear me? Your sexual advances are unwelcomed here." I teased before taking a bite of my chocolate croissant.

KoKo threw her head back and hooted with laughter. "Strictly dickly but hadn't had any for the past year? Your primary care doctor needs to prescribe some dick in your life."

"*A real one!*" Desi chimed in. I rolled my eyes at them both, as my two very immature friends high-fived.

"As a matter of fact, I got plenty of real dicks I could refer you to. Let me check my rolodex." KoKo continued, causing Desiree to damn near choke on her Chai tea.

Desi giggled. "You better leave Ivonne alone before she jump across this table. I'm way too pregnant to be trying to stop a fight today." Desiree joked.

KoKo snickered and waved her hands as if shooing the very thought of it away. "*Girl, bye!* I wish Ivonne *would.*" KoKo dared, staring me down while taking a sip from her straw.

She had a very serious look on her face and it was the rare times like these that I felt like I was back in high school. I could never tell if Koreen was joking or if this was a Miami-thing. Maybe this was the way women down here tested you, or maybe it was just a *KoKo* thing, feeling like she had something to prove.

"You know she's a lawyer, right?" Des reminded her playfully.

KoKo winked at me and smiled. "Ivonne knows I'm playing with her. I love her as much as I do my own blood sister."

"But you hate your sister." I reminded her. "Y'all don't even get along." I asked, confused.

"Exactly." She smirked, then gave me a playful punch. "You know I love fuckin with your bourgeois ass, bitch."

"Would you please refrain from calling me-" I started.

She quickly corrected her error. "My bad. I forgot. I meant to say bourgie ass *broad*." She corrected. "What time is it? I gotta get going. I have a rendezvous with the very exotic Moet this evening." She announced, glancing down at her iPhone.

"Moet? Is that the stripper chick?" Desi asked.

"No. For the last time, *Hennessey* is the stripper chick. Moet is Hennessey's sister and she *ain't* no stripper. Moet's an occupational therapist. I told y'all that already."

"What?" I laughed incredulously. "And her parents named her Moet?" Out of all the foolishness I had heard come out of KoKo's mouth this evening, this nonsense took the cake.

"*No.*" KoKo shook her head at me as if I were dense. "Y'all obviously don't listen to shit I say. I told you last week, her real name is Valerie. I nicknamed her Moet. Moet. Get it? *Mo' Wet?*" KoKo smirked.

"Really?" Desiree laughed and this time I joined her. "Didn't you hook up with her sister a month ago?" She asked.

I jumped in as I remembered something. "Wait, isn't she married?"

KoKo shrugged and gave Des and I a dirty look. "And?"

"Ok, I'm done." I shook my head in disgust. This was just too much. I gathered my newest blue Givenchy tote bag and stood up to leave.

"Me too. I gotta pick up the boys from my mom's house. I had to send her calls to voicemail three times since we sat down. I know she's ready for me to go get 'em." Desiree stated, slowly raising her pregnant body from her seat.

"Why can't *he* go get them?" KoKo asked. It was no big secret that KoKo despised Lucas. She never referred to him by his birth name. It was always "him", "his ass" or *"that nigga"*.

"Girl, I don't know where he's at and I don't care. Is it my turn to pay?" She asked, then slammed two twenty-dollar bills on the table before either of us could answer.

CHAPTER FOUR
KoKo

"Babe, you hungry?" Biggz asked nonchalantly, rubbing my soft bare ass, fully exposed beside him. I was sprawled out on his colossal-sized bed. He was sitting upright against the black leather headboard, rolling up a blunt. We had just been going at it like dogs and my mouth was too parched to speak, so I shook my head no instead.

This nigga had the nerve to have a look of grandeur and accomplishment as he watched me panting, no doubt thinking he had really put it on me. The reality was, I had just taken some new pills out on the black market. The side effect was severe dry mouth. The pills helped to heighten senses during sex and were well worth the dehydration.

After a few more seconds of trying to muster up enough spit to coat my throat, I was finally able to speak in an audible whisper. "Moet should be here in a few. She just text me."

He exhaled and released a puff of smoke before looking over at me, unbothered. "I ain't worried about that. As long you here wit' me, I'm gucci."

I hadn't exactly lied to Ivonne and Des about meeting up with Moet. I just left out the part about the threesome Biggz and I would be having *with* Moet. That was my business. My girls were just too judgmental. Especially Ivonne. Plus, it wasn't like they listened to shit I told them anyway. "You still got that money for me?" I asked Biggz seductively.

He passed the blunt to me. I eagerly grabbed it and took in a deep breath, allowing the herb's calming effect to travel through my body.

He reached over to grab a roll of money on the nightstand and handed it to me.

"This all of it?" I asked.

"It's what you asked for and extra, baby." He said.

I rose to my knees and gave him a quick peck on the lips and grabbed the cash.

"Who's yo' daddy?" He asked, slapping my ass so hard with a loud THWAP, I was convinced he left a handprint.

"*You my daddy.*" I purred.

"That's right. That's daddy's pussy." He boasted. THWAP! I cringed as he gave my ass another painful smack.

"You might as well just leave that nigga and come home to daddy."

Here we go again.

"And what about my daughter?" I asked hypothetically.

"She can come too. We going on, what, two years now–"

"Somethin' like that." I shrugged.

He continued, "Anyway, we've known each other a year and I still ain't met Jada. You know I love kids. You gon' have mine one day, mark my words."

I groaned inwardly. There was no way I was ever leaving Pierre or breaking up my family for Biggz or anyone else. There was definitely *no way* I was introducing my 2-year old big-mouthed daughter, J'adore, to anyone. Biggz was sadly under the impression that he was the only other man I was fuckin' with. *Wrong.* He didn't mind me messing around with other women, especially if he was able to participate, but he would become overzealous if I even seemed too chummy with artists in music videos. Biggz had even went as far as firing me from a video set he was directing because a reggae artist, a notorious playboy, would not keep his hands off of me during the shoot. Little did he know that Ganja Green, the reggae artist, and I still ended up hooking up after. As a matter of fact, Ganja and I hooked up whenever we were in each other's hometown.

However, Biggz accepted and nurtured my freak side and I loved him for it. Unlike Pierre, Biggz welcomed sex toys, costumes, whips, wax, and even threesomes. So I was filled with glee when the doorbell rung, announcing Moet's arrival.

"I'll get it, babe. It's Moet." I said. My c-cups bounced as I ran out the bedroom fully nude and to the front door.

"You made it!" I greeted. I gave her a kiss on the lips before letting her in.

She was definitely dressed for the part. Moet sported a black netted mini dress that exposed both her nipple piercings and black boy shorts. Last week, she was rocking large Jamaican braids. This week, she had her hair styled like mine; 20 inches of straight Brazilian hair that shined with each stride she took. She even had a part right down the middle like I had.

"You look nice." I said. "Are those Burberry?" I asked, eyeing the black four-inch platform heels she was sporting.

She stuck her right foot out, then turned it at an angle so I could get a better view. "*Yesss, honey!* I just got 'em two days ago. Aren't they cute?"

"Very." I agreed. "Girl, for a minute there I thought you had changed your mind about coming."

She laughed as I closed the door behind her. "*Hell naw!* I'm always down to make some extra cash."

I don't know why her statement bothered me. It stung. Yes, Moet was a married woman and a mother of a teenaged daughter and I *did* tell her that Biggz was willing to pay for this threesome. However, I was genuinely feeling Moet and I wanted her to feel the same for me. Moet was educated, freaky, and a good mother. She was classy and sophisticated, but she also knew how to let her hair down and let the hood side out... like me. I wasn't sure if she felt the same way about me or if I was just a temporary fling for her.

"Ooh, them nipples hard." She teased, staring at my chest. I looked down at my dark brown nipples resembling two large Hershey's Kisses. She gave both nipples a pinch, arousing me.

"*Mmmm*," I moaned. "I've been waiting on you all day. I'm ready to get this party started!" I shrieked, grabbing her hand and leading her to Biggz's master bedroom.

******

"Thought you said you were out with Desiree?"

Shit.

Pierre was already waiting for me when I finally pulled in the garage of our two-story home. He hadn't even waited for both my feet to cross the threshold before giving me the third degree.

"I was. I told you she wanted me to help her pick out some stuff for the baby."

Shit, shit, shit.

I had forgotten to give Des a heads up. She was supposed to have been my alibi. I almost chuckled when I caught myself silently praying. As if God listened to the prayers of cheaters.

"Don't Desiree have a litter of kids? All of a sudden she needs *your* advice? And why do you smell like cigarettes?" Pierre stood in front of our designer white leather furniture, staring at me with clenched jaws.

He folded his arms as he waited for an answer. He rarely let anyone upset him, but boy oh boy, when he did, it turned me on. His strong jawline looked even more pronounced and the way he peered into my eyes with his sexy bedroom eyes, as he was doing now, made me want to pounce on him

I tried my best to be casual as I kicked off my favorite black Giluseppe Zanotti stilettos; a gift from Biggz. I walked towards my fiancé and tried to give him a kiss on the lips. Pierre leaned his entire upper body away from me.

"Baby, Desi has five boys. This will be their first girl. We already have a daughter and Ivonne don't have any kids. Des just wanted my help. What was I supposed to say? *No?* She's my best friend. I don't know why you trippin'. You were okay with it when

I told you about it earlier." I furrowed by brows at him in feigned annoyance.

This time it was my turn to cross my arms as I awaited his response. I had purposely ignored his last question about the cigarettes. As hard as it was to believe, Pierre had never suspected that I was a closet smoker.

"I called you about fifty damn times and you didn't pick up." He stated.

"I left my phone in the Rover by mistake. I parked at Des' house and we rode to the mall together. By the time I realized that I had left my cell, we were already pulling up to the mall. I couldn't ask her to drive *all the way* back to her house to get my cell phone, Pierre." Inside, I was unnerved and praying like hell that he hadn't called Des looking for me.

Pierre remained silent. His dark brown eyes continued to peer deeply into mine, as if desperately searching for the truth. The silencce in the house was deafening, making it seem as if time were standing still.

Pierre finally shook his head slowly, causing his long thick locs to sway as he did so. Surprisingly, guilt was eating away at me. I felt like shit, but there was absolutely no way I was about to tell him that I had been too busy getting my pussy eaten by Moet and my ass fucked by Biggz to answer his calls.

Hell no.

I loved my man. Pierre was horrible in bed but he was still a damn good man to me and our daughter.

"Baby, I'm gonna be honest with you." I grabbed both his hand and looked him in his eyes. "I wasn't with Desiree today." I sighed. "I lied. I just needed some time alone. You know, some *me time*; away from everyone. I'm sorry baby. All I did was go to a massage parlor and then to a drive-in movie. I fell asleep watching the movie. I'm sorry I missed your calls." I said.

I loosened the knot around the waist of his sweatpants. "Let me make it up to you."

His face softened and he pulled me in and held me. "Nah, it's okay. You work hard. You deserve some me-time. I'm sorry for coming at you like that but please next time just let me know. I was worried about you and now Des is worried. She didn't know what the fuck I was talkin' about when I called her."

I gripped the imprint of my man's 9-inch dick again and kissed him sensually, wishing that I had gargled mouthwash after dining on Moet and Biggz.

"Come one, daddy. Let me make it up to you." I offered, falling to my knees. I attempted to pull down Pierre's pants but he caught both my hands.

"No, get up. You don't have to do all that and you know I hate when you call me that. It's weird." He stated, referring to my use of the word 'daddy'.

A feeling of defeat swept over me when he held out his hands to help me to my feet. I didn't let go of his hands. Instead, I used them to pull his rock-hard body close to mine. I shoved his thick locs out of the way with my forehead and began sucking in the skin on his neck ferociously. Pierre let out a soft moan and my pussy excreted in excitement. I grabbed his arms and laid his hands on my ass, hinting that I wanted my ass grabbed. Instead of grabbing a palmful of my firm bouncy ass like Biggz often did, his hands laid flat on them.

"*Fuck me right here, baby.*" I whispered breathlessly into his ear.

"What about J'adore?" He asked.

"Jada better be asleep. It's 11 o'clock."

"Why don't we just finish this in the bedroom?" He suggested.

I groped his dick again and gave him another passionate kiss. "Only if you promise to cum on my face." I purred seductively. My pussy pulsated at the memory of glob's of Biggz's thick white cum landing on the faces of both Moet and I just an hour ago.

"Don't talk like that, KoKo. I would never treat you like a ho', babe. You're the mother of my child. My soon-to-be wife. My queen." He said proudly.

I pulled away from him before letting out a loud sigh. This was the shit I was talking about. My man was a professional fitness trainer with the body of an Adonis and a dick the size of an elephant trunk, yet he refused to ravish my body sexually. I didn't always want to be made love to. I wanted straight, hardcore, kinky, animalistic *fucking* every once in a while. This was the reason why I stayed fucking around on his ass. I hadn't been satisfied in years and I was tired and bored of this shit.

"What's wrong?" He asked. I hadn't realized the exasperation had shown on my face.

Good, I wanted him to see that I was annoyed.

"I think I need to shower and lay down." I turned towards the direction of our spiral staircase.

"Alright babe, I'll meet you upstairs in a few." I rolled my eyes as he called out behind me.

CHAPTER FIVE
Desiree Loren

"Hello?"

"Is this Sofia?" I asked, knowing damn well it was that fat *puta*, Sofia.

"Who's asking?" She asked, hesitantly.

"*Puta,* you know who this is! Tell Lucas-"

"*Vete a la mierda*, Desiree! Why the fuck are you calling *my* phone?! Lucas isn't here, *bitch!*" She shouted into the phone, then hung up on me.

"Mommy, are you okay?" Sebastián, my six-year-old asked. He was the eldest of my 5 boys and very protective over me. He had reason to be concerned. My water had just broke and the baby wasn't supposed to be due for another four weeks.

"I think your baby sister is coming tonight so I'm going to the hospital. Your abuela is on her way to watch you guys. She only has one good leg so make sure you and your brothers behave. Got it?"

He nodded. "Got it. Is daddy coming home?"

It was a reasonable question. They boys hadn't seen their father going on three days now. I had no idea where the *idiota* was and he kept refusing to answer my calls, knowing I was in my third trimester with 5 rowdy boys to look after. The more I thought about it, the angrier I became.

KOKO

I sighed. "Don't worry about daddy. He's gonna meet me at the hospital. Remember the drill we practiced?"

He nodded.

"Good. Go put mommy's duffel bag by the door." I instructed.

"Do I have to call 911, too?"

"No. Ivonne's on her way, papi. Now go put the bag by the door."

I waited for Sebastián to leave my bedroom before calling my shitty husband again.

No answer.

I left another message. "Aye, listen you *hijo de puta*, my fucking water just broke and you're nowhere to be found. What type of father are you?! Is that bitch more important than your daughter?!" I hollered.

"*Que pasa*, Desi?" The sight of my mom startled me.

"Mami!" I cried out to her. She quickly hobbled over with her cane to where I was sitting on the bed.

"Is it the pain?" She asked.

"It's Lucas. I can't find him!" I sobbed.

She rubbed my back in a circle. "Lucas? How long has he been gone?"

"*Tres* - three days!" I answered between sobs.

"Have you checked the hospitals? Jails? Have you called the police?" She asked in Spanish. I could hear the concern in her voice.

I sniffled. "He's not in danger. He's with his whores!"

I felt my mother's body stiffen. "Desi, I told you not to marry that man. I told you find someone your own age, not-"

I held my hand up. "*Por dios, mami*! Not today! I don't wanna hear it!" I snapped.

"*Lo siento*, i'm sorry. I just don't like seeing you suffering like this. This wasn't the life that I wanted for you and your sisters, Desi." She explained.

Instead of becoming angry, I sobbed.

This was definitely not the future that I had hoped for either. I met Lucas when I was a senior in high school. I was running late to school and to make matters worse, the sky had started to turn gray. Flashes of lightening and rain drops warned me to put some pep in my step before I became a victim of the pouring rain. Seemingly, out of nowhere, a black Mercedes pulled over on the grass ahead of me.

"It's about to pour. Get in." An older well-dressed man, who looked to be in his mid-forties, stepped out of the black Mercedes. He was holding an oversized black umbrella, which he held up as walked around to the passenger side of the vehicle.

"Come on." He urged, as he held the door open.

I stopped in my tracks, no longer caring that my thick red curls were becoming damp by the rain.

"I don't even know you." I stated the obvious. He nodded. "You're right. You don't know me. Not sure if you know, but the radio just announced a tornado warning in the area. You're headed to the high school, right?"

"Why?" I asked, although it was obvious to see that I was lugging around a huge blue backpack.

KOKO

"Well, this whole area is under a tornado warning. I figured it'd be safer for you to be inside than walking under all of these trees during a severe thunderstorm." Lucas explained.

Years later he would admit that the whole tornado warning story had been a ploy to get me inside of his car.

Going against my better judgement, I entered the black Mercedes and would find myself regretting it ever since.

Knowing that my close friends and family would have strong opinions of our 30-year age gap, I managed to keep my relationship to Lucas a secret. I hadn't planned on ever telling my parents if I hadn't found out I was pregnant about six months after Lucas and I had met. Since I was so thin, I had been able to keep it a secret up until the day I gave birth to Sebastián.

My father basically disowned me for having a baby by a man older than he was. He called Lucas every foul name in the book, including a pedophile. My mother supported every one of my decisions, even when she didn't agree with my choice to accept Lucas' marriage proposal.

"This guy is no good for you, Desi. Won't you find someone your own age?"

"Mami, I love Lucas and he's the father of my son. He's doing the right thing by having us be a family." I tried explaining.

"Has he ever been married? What happened to his other wives? How many times has this guy been married?"

I didn't answer. Lucas had been man enough to admit to me that he had been married four times. In fact, the day he had met me, he had just separated from his fourth wife, but I wasn't about to tell my mother that.

"Just make sure you go to college, Desi. No more music videos. It's time for you to grow up and become a mom. You need to be a good example to your son. It's not about you and Lucas anymore. You have Sebastián now." Her advice had went in one ear and out the other.

Around that time, I had met Koreen Wilson while shooting a video in Costa Rica. We quickly became good friends once we realized that we had a lot in common, especially when it came to fashion. Ironically, KoKo had been the only person who liked Lucas back then. Now she despised him.

"Does he love you?" She had asked one evening while we were watching movies with Sebastián at her place.

"He tells me all the time he loves me." I answered.

"Saying he loves you and feeling it are two different things." She explained. "Do you feel it?"

"I think I do."

"Is he a good provider? Does he have any other kids?"

I took a second to think about it. "He has two other sons but they're grown."

"Does he make good money? He ain't no mooch is he?" She asked.

"No, he runs his own import and exporting business."

"Hunh?" She shot me a confused look.

I laughed. "He makes damn good money."

"So let's see: he loves you and Sebastián, he's not a mooch, and he's wealthy. I'd say you better marry that man. Plus, he's old. He'll be dead soon and you'll inherit his fortune."

I shook my head and laughed. *"You're horrible!"*

"*Shiid*, you better marry that man or I will."

CHAPTER SIX
Ivonne

I released a soft moan as the feel of soft wet kisses traveled up my flesh. Starting from my mountain of ass, to my slender back, and up the side of my neck.

Giggling uncontrollably, I managed to cry out, "Stop it, babe, that tickles!"

I was in mid-stretch when he used his large frame to his advantage, flipping me over effortlessly so that I was laying on my back. I smiled upon seeing him hovering over me, face to face, with each of his muscular arms acting as beams to support his 6-foot dark chocolate frame. His long locs became a curtain of African-rooted hair, hiding both our faces as he leaned in for a passionate kiss.

"I love you." I purred.

"And I love you more, Ivonka."

My insides felt like mush. I wanted to cry from happiness. The wait was finally over.

"What took you so long to find me? Never mind, you don't have to answer that. I'm just happy you're finally here now." I told him.

Our lips performed an encore as they met again for a long sensual kiss.

I unexpectedly shrieked with laughter, momentarily scaring him. "Babe, what in the hell is that?!" I pointed at the white flimsy paper bib tucked in neatly in his grey undershirt.

KOKO

"I've been waiting for breakfast." He informed, then commenced parting my honey-colored thighs before dining in.

RING-RING-RING. RING-RING-RING! RING-RING-RING.

The sound of my cell phone awoke me abruptly from my dream. I desperately wanted to go back to sleep and finish where I left off.

RING-RING-RING. RING-RING-RING! RING-RING-RING.

I wasn't sure if I was more upset that it was all just a dream or that someone was calling me back to back at six in the fucking morning.

With as much annoyance and attitude as I could possibly muster, I snatched my cell phone from my nightstand and shouted, "*Hello?!*"

"Damn, did I catch you at a bad time?" My long-time friend of 17 years queried. The fact that he knew me long enough to know better than to call me so early, really pissed me off even further.

"You know it's my day off. What do you want, Isaac?" I snapped.

"I have some great news. Guess who's moving to Miami?"

I pulled myself out of bed and headed towards the kitchen. I needed coffee. "I'm not in the mood for guessing games, Isaac. Just tell me."

"Remember when I told you that I put in a transfer with the company? Well..." He said.

"*Well...?*" I mocked him, still cranky.

"I was approved for the transfer!" He announced excitedly.

I tried to hide the glee in my voice. "Isaac, I told you that you didn't have to wait for a transfer to move down here. I have three guest bedrooms you could use until you got on your feet."

"I really wanted to keep my job."

"Isaac, you stock groceries at Walmart." I sighed.

"Look, I know you're not hurtin' for money but I'm a man. My father always taught me if a man doesn't work, he don't eat." He said pridefully.

"And this news couldn't have waited until after 8? I was having the best dream and you ruined it."

"There's another reason why I called…" He began.

"Okay." I said tentatively, then took a sip from my coffee mug.

"I need you to pick me up from the airport."

"Is that it? That could've waited."

"I'm at the Miami International Airport now."

Coffee spewed out of my mouth, spraying the top of the kitchen stove like a lawn sprinkler. "Are you serious? You have got to be fucking kidding me? A heads up would've been the considerate thing to do, you know? Unbelievable."

He laughed. "So, are you surprised? I wanted it to be a surprise." He added enthusiastically, clearly missing the irritation in my voice.

"What if I had company, Isaac? What if I was in the middle of getting some *ding*?" I asked. Ding was me and Isaac's code word for *dick*. For as long as I could remember, it was what we had always called it. "Dick", "cock", and "penis" sounded too harsh.

KOKO

"What if I was out of town with Desi and KoKo?" I resumed.

"Number one, you never have company."

"*Excuse me?*"

He continued. "And number two, you never leave the house. I know you're not doing anything."

"How in the hell would you know what I have going on over here? You're all the way in Louisiana."

"*Was* in Louisiana. Not anymore. Look, I gotta go. I see my luggage. I'll be waiting right outside in front of Terminal D." He quickly informed before hanging up.

Closing my eyes, I took in a deep breath, then exhaled. "Well ain't this a bitch." I said to myself.

Deep down, a feeling of excitement rose in my chest. Isaac Charles was *here*.

CHAPTER SEVEN
Ivonne

I purposely took my time applying my makeup and flat-ironed my shoulder-length mane before leaving the house to get Isaac. I wasn't getting all primped up for Isaac but for any possible prospects I could run into today. It was one of Steve Harvey's rules for single women. I had to always be prepared to bump into Mr. Right. If I had to be honest with myself, I knew that the competition out there was fierce. I was in my late 30s and I no longer had the body of younger women. Sure, I made it my business to work out at least twice a week, but the fact of the matter was that no one ever told me that getting older meant having a drastically slower metabolism. I had been a healthy and sexy size 6 all throughout high school and in my twenties. I was now a size 10 and could barely smell the aroma of pasta without gaining a few pounds. I can admit that my weight had somewhat contributed to how I viewed and felt about myself.

I pressed and slipped on a grey knee-length Chanel dress with big bright yellow polka dots and accentuated it with my favorite yellow Manolos. Today I was using a picture of first lady Michelle Obama as inspiration. I carefully clasped on my pearl necklace; an heirloom passed on to me from my nana. Nana Clementine had also left a hefty twenty-five million-dollar inheritance to me when she died. With my mom having been the only child and me being my mom's only child, it was my burning desire to one day have children to pass my inheritance on to.

My grandma Clementine had been a smart business-savvy shark. She had attended Howard University and earned a degree in finance as well as an MBA from UCLA. After working as an HR consultant at a small company for a few years, nana Clementine decided to take a leap of faith and quit her job to start her own HR consultant firm, I-Fix Management Consultant Group. The firm specialized in large corporate recruitment and cutbacks. My mother soon followed in her footsteps and is currently running the firm. They both were slightly disappointed when I decided to study law.

When I finally pulled up to Terminal D at Miami International, Isaac was pacing back and forth impatiently, with his bags resting on a bench. I blew my horn and pulled over from the congested lanes. If there was one thing I hated about moving to Miami, it was definitely the traffic and the impatient drivers. I popped the trunk of my Mercedes and turned on my hazard lights before stepping out the car to greet my closest friend of 17 years.

"I am so happy you're here!" I jumped in his arms to give him a hug, not caring that he was carrying two suitcases and had a duffel bag strewn across his shoulders. He seemed surprised at my gesture. Hell, I was surprised myself. I hadn't realized how much I missed him until now.

He hadn't changed much since I had last seen him two years ago. He was still short, muscular and the same shade of brown as Will Smith. He still had the same rugged appearance, looking like a black mountain man with a face full of facial hair. I was towering 2 inches over his 5-foot-6 frame. He had his long locs wrapped and covered in one of those Rastafarian-type beanies. As usual his clothes were not only wrinkled, but completely uncoordinated.

He dropped his luggage and gave me a tight hug. I thought I heard him inhale deeply, as his furry face nestled in my hair.

I pulled away from him. "You can put your bags in the trunk." I said before hitting the button on my key to release the trunk.

He took a look at my Mercedes C-class coupe and whistled. "Nice ride!"

"Thanks."

"Doesn't this car come out in 2 years?" He asked, sliding his stubby fingers over the yellow paint.

"Yep. Desi calls it the Bumblebee."

He nodded. "Figures you would get it in this color. Yellow was always your favorite color." He said, gently closing the trunk, then heading to the passenger door. I followed suit and jumped in the driver's seat.

"Speaking of your friends," Isaac started, "You think you can introduce me to KoKo? You know I've always had a huge crush on KoKo *'Koreen the Dream'* Wilson."

I laughed. "Just a word of advice: do *not*, under any circumstances, refer to KoKo as *Koreen the Dream*, unless you're ready to get your head knocked off." I warned.

KOKO

"Wow, she sounds like a bitch."

I wanted to tell him that she could be a major bitch most of the time, but instead laughed again. "I can introduce you to her, but don't get your hopes up. She's damn near married and out of your league." I didn't feel the need to disclose that being engaged meant nothing to KoKo. KoKo fucked whoever she pleased, whenever she pleased. She didn't care that she was putting herself and her family at risk. I couldn't help but feel a twinge of jealousy at times. Some women just didn't know how good they had it.

"Oh, so she's one of *those* type of women?" He said sourly.

"One of what type of women?" I asked, giving the car besides me the finger for not letting me cut in. The Hispanic looking dude looked straight ahead, pretended not to see me giving him the death stare.

"*Asshole!*" I shouted before speeding off.
I could see Isaac from my peripheral holding onto the door for dear life.

"Yo! Slow down, Vonne!"

I glanced at my speedometer. I was flying down the highway at 90 miles an hour. I slowed down to 75 miles.

"Welcome to Miami. Now finish what you were saying." I instructed.

"I don't remember. What *was* I saying before you damn near killed us?"

"About KoKo. You wanting to meet her. Her being out of your league." I tried jogging his memory.

"Oh yeah! She seem so down to earth and laid-back. I never thought she was one of those type of women."

"And what type of women are we talking about?"

A look of disgust covered his furry face. "You know exactly what I mean: gold-diggers, moochers, opportunists."

I quickly defended my friend. "I never said KoKo was a gold digger. She has her own money. If anything, people try to use *her* to meet celebrities. What I meant was be realistic, Isaac. Your lifestyle is totally different from KoKo's. Even if she wasn't engaged to Pierre, you simply couldn't afford to wine and dine her."

Again, Isaac didn't need to know that KoKo's engagement was nowhere near a deterrent to her *extracurricular* activities. It was simply none of his business and I didn't need him judging my friend any further.

"That's right, I forgot. Status and income are very important factors to the new millennium women nowadays." He fumed. I could feel the energy in the vehicle shift.

Oh god, I thought to myself. I really didn't feel like hearing another one of Isaac rants about how hard it was for him to find a good woman and how women nowadays were no longer looking for love.

"I swear it, Ivonne, every single woman I meet," He started, and I sighed, "They either looking for a man to help them pay their bills or move in to be a dad to their kids. And all of the educated and single independent women don't even wanna give a brother a chance because they think I have nothing to bring to the table." He ranted.

KOKO

I groaned as I switched lanes. I knew that was a personal jab at me. I silently thanked God that our exit was coming up.

He shook his head and continued, "I'm a good man, I have no kids, no babymomma drama, I'm employed, and I'm a gentleman. I'm different from all of these other cats out here."

I sighed for a third time. "You know how many men say that shit? Every man swears they're different and in that way you all are the same. Just be patient. There's no rush. I'm sure you'll find the right woman to settle down with." I said, feeling like a hypocrite.

CHAPTER EIGHT
KoKo

"Pierre, babe, I've been thinking..."

"Okay...?" Pierre peered at me curiously.

We were seated at *Le Duce* with an array of generous-sized slices of cake in front of us. My husband-to-be was a longtime vegan and Le Duce was the crème de la crème of vegan bakeries. With our busy schedule, Pierre and I had finally been able to keep a cake-sampling appointment.

"I've been thinkin' that maybe we should accept the offer?"

"For the reality show?"

I nodded meekly.

Pierre groaned. "Didn't we talk about this?"

"Think about it, baby. We could use the money to help pay for our honeymoon. Plus, it would give me a chance to focus on the wedding. We've pushed back the wedding, what, four times already? I don't have enough time to plan as it is. I still ain't find my dress yet."

He grabbed my hand. "The wedding isn't for another 13 months. You still got plenty time to find a dress."

I exhaled in frustration. "It's just a wedding special, babe. Don't you think it's a good opportunity to be able to get paid to do something we need to do anyway? I wouldn't have to fly out so much and

KOKO

work so hard the whole year. I'd be able to just focus on our wedding." I pointed out.

Pierre released his hand from mine. "Babe, I already told you, you don't have to work. You *choose* to work. I can take care of us. I asked you after you had J'adore, to just stay home and take care of the household."

I shook my head. There was no way I was gonna be a miserable stay-at-home mom like Desi. Desiree and I had met on the set of a reggaetón video shoot years ago in Costa Rica. Once she married that sorry ass nigga and became a housewife, her life changed for the worse. I regret ever encouraging her to marry that sorry ass nigga. I couldn't fathom the idea of me as a stay-at-home mom. I was addicted to the fame and the money. Secondly, I was used to a certain lifestyle that Pierre could not simply afford on a fitness trainer's salary. Yeah, he trained and worked for A-list celebrities, but I was still bringing in 5 times the amount he was.

"Didn't you say reality TV cursed your last marriage?" He asked.

"That was different. The show would only be about us planning our wedding. Not drama or scandal. Big difference." I stroked his chin. "Just think about it, baby. That's all I'm askin'. I can have Ivonne look over the contract and see what she think."

I could tell he was still apprehensive. "I just don't think it's a good idea, Koreen. I don't want Jada being exposed to that."

"J'adore is *two*! We would only be filming for one season, Pierre. It's just a wedding special, not a 3-year contract like *Koreen Unfiltered*."

Pierre let out a deep sigh. His long dark locs swayed as he shook his head. "I don't know, babe. Have Ivonka look at the contract but don't sign anything until we talk about it again. I'm really not feeling it, though, KoKo. I have a bad feeling about this and my gut is usually right."

I nodded, but in the back of my mind, I knew that I would get him to sign that contract. We needed that fuckin' money. This wedding was costing us a small fortune.

Buzzzzzzzzzz! This was the fourth time my phone had vibrated since Pierre and I arrived at Le Duce. I glanced at my iPhone, already predicting that it was either Biggz or my booking agent, Irene.

Can't stop thinkin about u. Send me a pic, babe.

I was wrong. It wasn't Biggz or Irene. It was Moet. A few seconds later, my phone vibrated again as a I received a picture message from Moet. It was a picture of her with nothing but long braids and a pair of red Jimmy Choos.

"Who's that?" Pierre asked.

"Irene." I lied nonchalantly. I placed my phone on silent and dropped it in my red Alexander McQueen handbag; another gift that Biggz had showered me with.

Pierre stared at me pensively.

"What?" I asked in defense. In the four and a half years that we had been together, Pierre had never outright accused me of being unfaithful. He loved me and J'adore to death. It was almost as if I could do no wrong in his eyes and I loved him even more for that.

"You know, it's been awhile since me and you have gone anywhere." He answered.

I tilted my head up as I reflected on what he'd just said. "We just left Jamaica 3 weeks ago." I reminded him. R&B singer, Tristan Greene, had shot a video in Kingston that I had had the pleasure of modeling in. Since Pierre had trained Tristan for a recent blockbuster film, he offered my fiancé to come along; all expenses paid.

"I meant just the two of us. Without Jada, any assistants, or a group of people. You should see if your mother can watch Jada, so we can catch a play at the amphitheater."

"Alright. When?"

"Tonight." He answered.

"*Tonight?*"

"Yes, tonight since we're both off today. It's not often that we have the same off-days. Call her now and see what she says. If not, I'll see if one of my sisters can babysit."

I groaned inwardly. I was supposed to be meeting up with Biggz immediately after our cake-sampling.

"I wish you would've mentioned it earlier, Pierre. I already told Irene I would do a last-minute photo-op for that new urban denim line." I lied. "Let's just reschedule. I'm off Monday."

"Can't. I'm training Armani Rayne all day Monday. Can't Irene reschedule the shoot?"

"Armani? The singer?" I asked, intrigued. I couldn't help feeling a twinge of jealousy. If I weren't so secure in my relationship with my man, I would have probably had a fit. Armani Rayne was a bad bitch with vocals and an alluring aura to match.

"Yeah. Thought I told you. She hired me a few weeks ago. I train her on Mondays."

I feigned a look of disappointment. "See what I mean, baby? This is why I said we should do the reality show. I would be able to take a break from shoots and club appearances and still get paid by the network. I wish I could cancel the photoshoot, but I already agreed to it." I lied again. "If I don't do it, they'll get someone else. I really need the exposure."

Pierre looked taken aback. "And you don't think you have enough exposure? Look!" His index finger pointed towards the front windows of Le Duce. Ripples of flashes greeted us as the paparazzi aimed their cameras in our direction.

"*Vous aimez?*" I was grateful for the interruption brought on by Madame Duce's old Haitian ass. I wasn't about to agree to see a boring ass play with Pierre. That was another minor problem in our relationship. We had *nothing* in common. He was an earthy vegan who didn't smoke, drink, loved neo-soul music, and was also into that weird new age spirituality. I, on the other hand, was a closet-smoker, grew up Pentecostal, was into fashion, and most importantly, loved me some pork!

My fiancé answered Madame Duce. "*Le gateau est magnifique.*" I hadn't a clue what they were saying. I didn't speak French but Pierre did. He was also fluent in Spanish, Haitian-Creole, and Portuguese. It was because of him that Jada was also picking up foreign languages.

"We're gonna go with these two." I pushed both the white almond and lemon coconut slice of cake forward.

"*Très bien.*" She was grinning from ear to ear, no doubt excited about the buzz and free publicity we were creating at her establishment.

***

"I seen you and your ol' man, the other day. Coming out of a cake shop. Dude looked stiff as fuck." Biggz laughed.

"You seen us?" I asked. My worse fear was running into Biggz, Moet, or Ganja, while I was out with my family. I was also starting to feel like two different people. Like I was living a double life.

I was chilling with Biggz on the set of a music video that he was directing. The artist was a brand-new rap artist who had wanted me in his video, but I had flat-out declined. I didn't do videos for artists who were nobodies. I was sure he couldn't afford to hire me, anyway.

"I seen you with that lame ass nicca. I almost socked the shit out of him." The cigar between Biggz teeth shook as he guffawed.

The shit wasn't funny to me.

"I'm jokin'. Nobody's gonna hurt ya' boy, but I did see y'all on Entertainment Tonight. I didn't even know you got engaged on me, shorty." He sounded hurt.

"Does it matter?" I asked.

It was a lot that he didn't know. I had been engaged since the first day that I met Biggz, but it wasn't none of his damn business. Shit, he probably had a whole wife and family that he was keeping from me.

"Of course, it matters, Koreen. Believe it or not, I love you. I only put up with this shit because I'd rather have some of you than none of you. As long as you're not fuckin with anybody else then I'm cool."

"When are y'all going on lunch?" I asked, changing the subject. I hated when he started talking like this.

"You hungry? I'll get one of the P.A.'s to bring you some food. Yo!" He snapped his right finger, signaling one of the production assistants.

"Wait." I quickly pulled down his arm. "It's not food that I want." I smirked mischievously.

"*Shiid*, I'll send everyone on a lunch break now. LUNCH BREAK! ONE HOUR!" He instructed the crew.

In ten minutes tops, we were in his trailer and on an ancient couch. Biggz was on top of me pumping away while drops of sweat were falling down his chin and landing on my chest.

I released a deafening moan as Biggz continued pumping his massive curved dick in and out of me in rapid motions.

"*This my pussy?*" He asked between grunts.

"Yesss, daddy it's yoooours!" I replied. He brought his head towards mine and our tongues kissed.

"I'm 'bout to cum." Biggz whispered. "You want it?"

I nodded.

KOKO

He slid his dick out of me and began stroking it up and down until my belly was covered in his semen.

CHAPTER NINE
Desi

"KoKo, could you quit hogging the baby? I wanna hold her too." Ivonne lamented.

"Aww she is so cute, Desi! What's her name?" KoKo asked, ignoring Ivonne.

"Delilah."

"*Aww.*" KoKo and Ivonne cooed in unison.

"Delilah. I love it. It's cute." Ivonne stated over KoKo's shoulder, making faces at the baby. "Can I hold her now?"

"Alright, alright. Sit down so I can put her on your lap." KoKo instructed.

Ivonne looked insulted. "I know how to hold a baby, KoKo. Just give me the baby." She said, holding her arms out.

KoKo held Delilah closer to her. "How would you know how to hold a newborn? You don't have any children."

Ouch. Sometimes KoKo was just mean for no reason. She knew motherhood was a sensitive subject for Ivonka.

"I've held babies before, KoKo. Stop being a bitch. Let me hold her." Ivonne's voice was full of confidence but her eyes didn't lie. She looked pained.

"You might've held babies before but she's a newborn. I didn't say you couldn't hold the baby.

KOKO

Just sit your ass down so I can give her to you." She replied firmly.

I quickly interfered. "KoKo, give Ivonne the baby. It's almost feeding time and the lactation nurse is gonna be here soon."

KoKo rolled her eyes as Ivonne gently grabbed my daughter away from KoKo, then took a seat on my bed.

KoKo glanced around the room. "Sooo, where's what-his-face? Did that nigga even show up?" She asked, looking disgusted.

I didn't even bother answering. I couldn't answer because I had no clue where Lucas' ass was. I didn't wanna admit it, but I was low-key worried that something might've happened to him. He had never missed the birth of any of our other children.

"Speaking of the devil." KoKo rolled her eyes at Lucas as he waltzed in. "I think it's time for me to bounce. Bye Delilah." She made kissing noises at the baby before leaving.

Lucas looked confused. "*Que es esta? Delilah?*" He walked over to Ivonne and our newborn daughter. "I told you Mariela, after my mother."

"*¡Chinga tu madre!* Fuck your mother!" I spat. Both Lucas and Ivonne were stunned.

"*¡Chinga tu madre!?*" Lucas asked.

"That's right. Fuck her!" I repeated. "And fuck you! I been calling your mother all day and she's been ignoring my calls. Fuck her."

"She didn't answer because she knew you were looking for me! She said you been calling her for three days straight! She got tired of answering your calls!"

"Where the fuck were you Lucas? Did you not get my texts? I had to call Ivonne to bring me to the hospital. Your bitches more important than your daughter?"

"Did I say that?!" He asked, raising his voice. "*Mierda*! This is why I don't stay home! All you do is bitch and complain, woman!"

Ivonne stood up and handed the baby to me. "I think I'm gonna head out now, Des. Call me if you need me." She said uneasily.

"I'm so sorry, Vonne. I'll call you." I said, feeling remorseful.

"Don't worry about it." She gave me an awkward smile.

"Thank you, Ivonka, for bringing her to the hospital." Lucas said and Ivonne nodded politely, then exited the room.

I returned my attention back to Lucas. "So? Where were you?"

Lucas sighed, then slicked back his graying hair with both palms before taking a seat on the chair across from me. "In jail."

"Bullshit."

"I'm telling you the truth. Ask Martin." He said, referring to his younger brother. "I had to call him to bail me out."

"What happened?"

"Driving with a suspended license." He answered, looking everywhere around the room but at me.

He was lying and I knew I would have to find out on my own later. As for now, I was going to enjoy my newborn baby girl. Maybe Delilah was a blessing in disguise. Perhaps now that Lucas had a daughter of his own, it would open his eyes to the errors of his ways.

CHAPTER TEN
Ivonne

In a lot of ways, Isaac Edward Charles II and I were a lot alike. Like me, he was an only child, as was both his parents. He too grew up with a silver spoon in his mouth. The only difference between our families were that his had filed for bankruptcy when Isaac was a freshman in high school. Mine hadn't. His father had won a multi-million-dollar lottery ticket right before Isaac was born. Mr. Charles had done the right thing and made a few investments in some stocks and bonds and had plans to start a vegan fast food chain. Unfortunately, before he could create a business plan, Mr. Charles was diagnosed with breast cancer. He died shortly after. His mom remarried about a year after to a low-down scheming career criminal who not only sold every stock, but also spent every dime of the family fortune. He filed for a divorce once the money ran out. The experience left Isaac very bitter and it was during the time that he was adjusting to his new life as the son of a single mother on government assistance that we had met.

It was the fall of my freshman year in high school and I was dating Francois Lewis, the cutest guy on Jon Batiste High's basketball team. Despite the fact that Francois came from "new money", which was wealth recently acquired, he was still the most handsome and popular boy at our high school. I felt lucky to be on his arm every morning when he walked me to class. Not only did he have the dreamiest green eyes, he was also a sophomore which meant he had a car. One Friday night, on our way to a house party, Francois pulled up to an Amoco gas station to buy a pack of Trojans in a rough part of town. I stayed in the car and locked my door as I waited on Francois to come back out. I fiddled with the radio dial and stopped when I heard my favorite Babyface song. Francois finally returned as the song was ending.

"What took you so long?" I asked.

"Remember that kid whose dad died last year?" He asked as he shifted the gears of his Mercedes.

"Uh.... yea, what's his name again? Ivan?" I asked.

"Isaac. I ran into him inside." He answered, peeling out of the gas station like a mad man.

"Right, Isaac. He lives around here now? Did you speak to him?" I asked, intrigued.

"We spoke. Bought some trees from him. He goes to Phyllis Wheatley High. He says he hates it. I invited him to the party. You think Mozelle will mind?" He asked.

I shook my head no. As long as Isaac mentioned that he had been invited by Francois, no one would give him a hard time. I was more taken aback by the fact that the quiet nerd who had once been in my advanced calculus class was now on the corner selling illegal drugs.

Francois continued, "Its fucked up how his stepdad fucked them. Running off with his dad's money."

"I thought they said they lost all of their money." I stated confused.

"Psshh! I doubt it. His old man was loaded. He won the 150 million-dollar Powerball. There's no way."

When we finally arrived at Mozelle's party, Francois started drinking right away. By the time Isaac had made it, Francois was sloppy drunk. Francois was so plastered, he decided that he would publicly taunt and humiliate Isaac, although he had been the very one to invite him.

"Hey who invited you to the party? Didn't you hear? No beggars allowed." Francois words slurred, cornering a confused looking Isaac in the kitchen. A few cheerleaders and jocks laughed.

I pulled at Francois's varsity jacket. "Francois, chill out. You invited him, remember?" I reminded him.

"Fuck him! He's nothing but a pauper. Why don't I ask Mozelle to hire you to clean up this place after we trash it? You know, since you need the money and all." Francois was now swaying from side to side while still holding on to his can of Corona. Someone had decided to bring five cases of Corona and from the looks of it, Francois had consumed almost an entire case by himself.

"I'm outta here." Isaac said angrily as he headed towards the backdoor.

"You're not going anywhere until this place is spotless." Francois said belligerently, grabbing the back of Isaac's gray hoodie.

I was deeply embarrassed. Not only for Francois, but for Isaac as well.

When Isaac made eye contact with me, I looked down, pretending to look for something near my brown Nine West leather boots.

"Let go of me, Francois. I don't want any problems. I just wanna leave." Isaac tried to reason.

"Yo, Julien! Marc!" Francois called out to his teammates, who were also in a drunken stupor. "Find a chair and rope. We're gonna tie this beggar up like a slave until the party is over."

Again, Isaac's eyes met mine in alarm.

"Guys, wait." I finally spoke up. "Let go of him." I ordered Julien and Marc, who were holding him with his arms behind his back as if he were under arrest.

Both boys glanced at Francois, waiting for orders. Francois stumbled as he made his way towards me.

"What, you got a thing for beggars, now?" He pointed an elbow at Isaac.

I crinkled my brows in disgust. "What? No. I just think what you guys are doing is lame. You all need to grow up."

"I don't know." Francois started, "You sure were asking a lot questions about him on our way here." Isaac and I made eye contact again, awkwardly.

"Don't be ridiculous, Francois. You were the one who invited him."

Francois continued on with his taunt. "What, you tryna fuck this bum tonight?"
SLAP!

Before I could even stop myself, I slapped the shit out of Francois. Francois surprised me by slapping me right back.

"Yo!" Isaac shouted, releasing himself from Marc's and Julien's grasp. He charged head first at Francois. I watched in horror as both boys began fighting and as Julien and Marc jumped in.

CHAPTER ELEVEN
Ivonne

"I've been dating this guy."

Isaac and I were sprawled out on my living room floor in our pj's watching a Kevin Hart's stand-up special.

"I know." He said casually.

"Hunh? How?"

"Hardly ever here. I'm surprise you're home tonight."

"What? That's not true."

He shrugged. "Okay." He said. For as long as I'd known Isaac, he never wasted energy debating with me or anyone else. Most of the time it really irked my nerves.

"Don't you wanna know his name?"

"Not particularly." He answered dryly.

"I really believe he's the one."

"How long have you known him?"

"Tomorrow will make it two weeks. Now, before you say anything-"

"I wasn't gonna say anything." He interjected. "Just be careful, that's all."

"I thought you weren't gonna say anything."

He laughed. "I *didn't*. All I said was be careful. You're a grown woman. I can't tell you what to do."

I nodded. "That's true."

"Where'd you meet this one?"

"At a gas station. It's actually a funny story."
He nodded.
"*What?*" I asked suspiciously.
He laughed again. "I didn't say anything!"
"But you want to. I know you do."
"At least it's not one of those dating apps you're always prowling. I will give you that much credit. You just always seem to rush into things when you're dating. Just let things run their natural course." He explained.

"That's not true."
"Last guy you were talking to, Derrick-"
"Darren." I corrected.
"Okay, Darren. What happened with him?'
I shrugged. "I don't know. We just stopped talking."
"Because?"
"I was ready to take it to the next level and he wasn't."
"Y'all hadn't even been talking for that long, Ivonne. Just learn to enjoy the moment for what it is and let everything run its course. You can't control everything."
"But I'm going on 38 this year." I reminded him.
"Okay?"
"I wanna get married and have kids, too, you know." I admitted, although this hadn't been his first time hearing me confess my fears.
"You will."
"How do you know?" I asked, desperately needing reassurance that I would one day have my happily ever after.

"I just know. Now, watch the show."

"You better not get married before me, Isaac." I threatened, selfishly. "If you do, -"

"*Watch the show.*" He repeated more firmly.

No matter what Isaac thought, I knew Adrian Michaels was the man I had been waiting for my entire life. He worked as a chemist, had sole custody of his seventeen-year-old daughter, and was *fine as hell*. After days of phone calls and texting, we agreed to meet at Trendy Indies.

"So why is a smart, successful, and attractive woman such as yourself single, Ms. Ivonka?" He asked two weeks ago.

I chuckled nervously. "I could ask you the same."

"True enough." He smiled. "However, I was married before for thirteen years and we had a daughter together. You've never been married and managed to not have any children."

I shrugged uncomfortably. I didn't know why I was nervous. It was a question most men asked. Perhaps I was just so enchanted with the fact that Adrian was such a good catch, that I wanted to pass all of his questions.

"You don't have to answer that. Just wanna make sure you're not crazy." This time he let out an uncomfortable chuckle.

I wanted to cease all doubts about me, so I answered. "No, it's fine. I completely understand. The truth is I've always put my education and career first. Unfortunately, that meant my relationships suffered, being in the backburner and all." That wasn't exactly the truth. The *real* truth was I had never been in a relationship longer than six months and I didn't know why. I had started to believe that maybe it was me. Perhaps I was the problem.

Adrian took a sip of his cup. "And you think you're ready to settle down now?"

I smiled. "I know I'm ready now." I said, feeling like I was interviewing for the role of his next wife.

He nodded. "Good, good. As I've told you before, Ivonka, I'm not looking for a piece of ass nor am I looking to play games. I'm looking to settle down and remarry." Those words were like music to my ears.

"Same here."

"What kind of men are you looking for?" He asked.

"Ummm...hmmm...that's a good question." I tapped my index finger against my chin while I tried to think. *What was my type?*

"I need a woman who knows what she wants. I need to know I'm the man she's been waiting for. Know what I mean?" Adrian asked.

You're definitely what I been waiting for. I wanted to say but didn't wanna come across as "thirsty".

I nodded instead. "Yep, I definitely understand. I do know what I'm looking for. I don't ask for much. Just want a guy who's employed, responsible, loving, and who respects me."

"So lemme guess, he gotta fit a certain income bracket, too?"

I instantly thought of Isaac. "Not, not necessarily." I lied. "As long as he's employed."

"Sounds simple enough. Still can't believe a woman as fine as you single. Never been with a woman with some pretty green eyes, either. Got me feeling like I hit the jackpot over here." He laughed.

I blushed. "Thank you."

"No, thank *you*."

I blushed again. "What type of woman are you looking for?" I asked, before taking a sip of my iced coffee.

"Someone who's loyal, who will have my back through the good and the bad. Umm, gotta be self-sufficient, classy...gotta be able to let me lead-"

"What do you mean by that?" I asked.

"Well, I grew up a southern Baptist. I also grew up with a father in the house. He wasn't my biological father, but raised me since I was two. That man did more for more than my own father ever did, so in my eyes, he's my father. Anyway, being brought up in the church, we were taught that the men were the head of the house-"

I interjected. "I don't see anything wrong with that."

He continued. "My mother allowed my father to make all the decisions. She allowed him to be a man. Most women nowadays, especially these new age independent women, they act like they don't need a man. Everyone needs someone."

Not knowing how I should respond, I simply nodded in agreement.

Adrian continued, "And majority of 'em can't cook! Can you cook?"

I nodded again. "I can cook." I lied. I had never cooked anything except for a pot of hard-boiled eggs and I had only done it to help Desiree prepare for an Easter egg hunt. I didn't want to admit to Adrian that

I had grown up with full-time cooks and that even my mother had never learned to cook. I currently had a full-time cook. However, it didn't matter. I would make it my business to enroll in cooking courses and dismiss Stefan, my cook, as soon as I learned how to prepare enough meals. Maybe I could even get Stefan to teach me.

"Really? What do you cook?"

I laughed nervously. "Well, you know, the basics and a few other stuff. I work a lot of hours so I hardly have enough time to cook."

"I cook as well. Maybe on our next date, I'll cook for you." He suggested.

Yes! A second date! I congratulated myself.

"I would love that." I answered nonchalantly.

Inside, I jumped for joy. I had passed Adrian's test!

***

"So, when we meeting this new guy? What's his name again? Omar?" KoKo asked. She was laid out on Desiree's bed, in a way-too-short yellow summer dress. Desi and I had just entered Desi's bedroom after checking on Delilah. Her mom had the boys and Lucas was God knows where, leaving Desi to tend to their newborn baby alone.

"His name is Adrian. I don't know if I want him meeting you crazy hussies." I teased, leaning against the wall near the door.

"Does he know about Isaac?" Desi asked, lying down on the bed beside KoKo.

KoKo squinted, then lifted her head from the bed. "Wait, who the fuck is Isaac?"

Desiree answered before I could. "Ivonne's best friend."

"*What*? I thought *we* were Ivonne's best friends."

Again, Desi replied before I could explain. "No, Isaac is her bestie from back home."

KoKo let out an exaggerated gasp. "I didn't think she had any friends back in Baton Rouge." She said to Desiree, as if I weren't even standing there.

Desi nodded. "Yep and supposedly he's been in love with Ivonka since like high school or somethin'. High school, right, Ivonne?" Desi looked at me for confirmation.

"Isaac is like a brother to me and no, I haven't told Adrian about him yet." I said.

"I'm so confused." Said KoKo. "Why the hell do you need to tell dude about Isaac?"

Desi interjected. "Because Isaac just moved to Miami a couple of days ago. I think he flew down last Thursday, right, Ivonne?"

"Satur-'" I started to say.

"*Right*! Saturday!" Desi exclaimed. "So anyway, Isaac and Ivonne over there shacking up now."

"*Wooooord*?" KoKo asked dramatically, with her eyes bucked wide open.

I laughed incredulously. "Hold up! Isaac and I are *not* shacking up. I told him he could stay with me until he found a place. I'm hoping he'll find a place soon. That way I won't even have to mention anything to Adrian."

"Back to Isaac." KoKo started, "Is he fine? How old is he? Does he come from money, too?"

Desi waved a hand at KoKo dismissively. "Girl, you don't want him. He works at Walmart."

KoKo groaned. "No wonder she don't want his ass."

"He's still a good guy." I said defensively, feeling the need to stick up for my friend. "And he wants to meet you, KoKo."

"Tell him to get in line." She said, laying her head back on the bed.

Desi laughed.

I shook my head. "See, this is why I don't want Adrian meeting neither of you."

Desi looked taken aback. "What'd I do? KoKo said that. I didn't do anything."

I smirked. "You encourage her to act out."

KoKo raised an arm in the air. "Okay, *fine.* I'll meet your friend Isaac and I'll TRY to be nice."

"I need you to do a lot more than try, please." I replied.

"I just wanna meet the new boo." Said Desi.

"Speaking of boos," KoKo began, "Antwon told me that you've been giving him the cold shoulder, Ivonne. You won't answer his calls and you been ignoring his text messages."

Desiree busted out laughing and KoKo joined her. Desi's laugh was so infectious, that sometimes it was hard not to laugh with her. We all knew why she was laughing. There was no way that I was ever giving Antwon the time of day. I was also never allowing KoKo to set me up with one of her sketchy 'friends' ever again.

"Now you know you did Ivonne wrong, KoKo." Desi said.

KoKo smiled. "I ain't did *shit*."

Desi laughed again. "Out of all the rich eligible bachelors that you know, you hook Ivonne up with the kush man?"

KoKo hooted in laughter. "It was just a joke! You could've gotten a lifetime supply of free weed."

"You know I don't smoke that shit and even if I did, he still isn't my type."

"Now you're being selfish. Desi and I smoke. Stop thinking about yourself, wench. Spread the wealth." KoKo said and they both giggled.

I shook my head. "It isn't funny. I went shopping and got all dressed up to meet him. I had to beg Marie to schedule me a last-minute appointment because I thought Antwon ..." I didn't even know how to finish my thought.

Desiree and KoKo howled with laughter. "At least he was cute." KoKo said.

"Maybe to you, not to me." I said.

KoKo smiled mischievously. "I told you, you should've just fucked him. When was the last time you had some?"

"Did you already give it up to Adrian?" Desi asked.

I smiled.

KoKo looked astonished. "You already fucked new dude? That's what's up." She sounded proud.

"Why do you seem surprised? You give it up on the first date all the time." I pointed out.

KoKo shrugged. "Yeah, but that's different. I'm not trying to marry these niggas. I got a man."

"That's beside the point." I said, not knowing what else to say.

KoKo continued. "Just don't start disappearing on us like you always do whenever you find yourself a man."

"That part." Desi chimed in, in agreement.

"And you," KoKo said, turning her attention to Desiree.

Desi sat up. "What about me?" She asked defensively.

Oh Lord, I thought to myself. "KoKo, please don't start with her. She just had a baby." I reminded.

"Damn, calm down. I was only gonna ask if you needed us to sleep over tonight. Since yo' nigga nowhere to be found and all."

"Nah, I think I'm good. Delilah's a good baby."

"You sure?" I asked, although I didn't really feel like sleeping over. I was hoping to sleep at Adrian's tonight. In fact, I had been sleeping over at his house almost every night, since the night after we met up.

"Positive." She assured.

"So, guess what?" KoKo asked us.

"What?" Desi and I replied together.

"I think Valerie's been stealin' from me."

"Who's Valerie?" I asked.

KoKo released an exaggerated sigh. "Valerie is Moet, remember?"

"Why don't you just call her Valerie then? Makes it less confusing."

KoKo continued, dismissing my complaint. "Anyway, I don't know how I should go about asking her."

"What do you mean she been stealin' from you?" I asked. "Stealing what?"

KoKo sat up. "So y'all know that I pop a couple of pills. One for recreational use and the other one is prescribed."

I asked, "What is it? Oxy?"

She nodded. "Right."

"Wait, you still taking that?" I asked, concerned.

I had been under the impression that her back issue had been long resolved five years ago.

She held up her palm. "Look now, let's not make this about me. Can I finish?"

I nodded. "Fine, go ahead."

"So anyway, I take my pills everywhere. I can't leave 'em home because I don't want Jada getting into them. Plus, Pierre don't need to know about 'em."

"I'm sure he doesn't." I rolled my green eyes, then glanced at Desi, waiting for her to giggle in agreement. Instead, she was unusually quiet.

KoKo cocked her head to the side. "Are you gonna let me finish or nah?"

I didn't say anything.

Again, Desi was quiet.

KoKo continued, "So anyway, I been missing entire bottles from my purse. These pills cost money. I don't know how the fuck I should even ask her about it. I'm about to just stop fuckin' with her thievin' ass."

"Unless you're certain it's Moet, I wouldn't mention it. I would just stop seeing her for a while and see if they continue to come up missing." I suggested.

KoKo threw up her hands in frustration. "Who the fuck else could it be? Other than you guys, she's the only other person that I'm with almost every day."

"What about Biggz?" I asked.

"What the fuck would Biggz need to steal for? He's rich as fuck and got his own stash."

I shrugged. "I don't know, KoKo. I'm just trying to be helpful."

"Well stop cus you sounding crazy."

KOKO

CHAPTER TWELVE
Desi

I'm seven months pregnant with my seventh child and high on Oxycodone. If that weren't bad enough, I'm also contemplating if tonight is the night I finally jump off the balcony of this ridiculously large three-story mansion.

My five rowdy boys and Delilah are already fast asleep and as usual, my husband, Lucas, is out running the streets at the wee hours of the morning. The only person keeping me company at the moment is Lauryn Hill's Ex-Factor. My broken spirit yearns to cry out in desperation for help, as I listen to Ms. Hill crooning my life with her song.

With my chest tightening in frustration, I reflect on how the end of my life is about to play out. A stream of hot tears bursts through, tumbling past my butterscotch-colored cheeks, and joins the snot sliding onto my quivering lips. My long frizzy red curls, the same red curls that have been my crowning glory since the days of my youth, the cause of many childhood fights in the Havana projects, the inheritance passed down to me from my Cuban mother, Scottish grandmother, and Bahamian father, currently mimics that of a wild biracial Frankenstein. Though it's the middle of a humid summer night in Miami, a trail of goosebumps pricks along my arms and legs, reminding me that I've been wearing this blue lace teddy since 10 pm last night, waiting on Lucas' ass to come home. It's now after 4 a.m.

Despite the fact that I'm shivering on the ledge of a multimillion-dollar mansion, one step away from the end of me and my unborn daughter's existence, I can't stop thinking about how I fucked up my life. My biggest regret at 24 years old, is being tied down since the age of 18 by having all these kids so early, and getting married to a man three times my age. An old, lying, manipulative motherfucker, at that.

Taking in a deep breath, I ask for God's forgiveness as I finally come to a decision. The last thing I can remember hearing is my husband's voice behind me shouting for me not to jump. I laugh as I purposely leap off the ledge towards freedom.

As often as I've tried, I could never bring myself to tell my best friends that I had reoccurring dreams of me jumping off the ledge of my bedroom balcony. In each dream, Lucas would walk in right before I would leap off. I always felt happy as I plummeted to my death.

The feeling to die had become so overwhelmingly powerful that I had tried to hang myself with bedsheets one evening while the children were vacationing in Columbia with Lucas' parents. I had been seven months pregnant with Delilah and if Lucas hadn't come home when he did, I wouldn't be here. I wasn't sure if he had even realized that I was high and drunk. He had been so shaken up after that incident, that he insisted on staying by my side for two days. *Two days.* That was an incident that he insisted that we keep just between the two of us.

What I couldn't understand was, if he knew about my depressive state, why would he just disappear on me? Did he not give a fuck about me or even his fucking kids? Yes, I had been stealing bottles of pills from KoKo and I didn't feel a hint of remorse about it. I hated my life, I hated Lucas, and sometimes I even hated my friends. Ivonne, with her wildly successful career and affluent upbringing. KoKo and her perfect little family that she continued to take for granted. If I didn't have a conscious, I would have set up Koreen a long time ago so that Pierre's naïve ass would finally catch her. She didn't deserve him. However, my girls were like family to me. I refused to worry them with my problems. Besides, most people didn't really wanna bother with people who were depressed. Yeah, everyone always says *"I wish he or she would've reached out to me"*, after someone commits suicide, but I don't think people really take depressed people seriously until it's too late.

CHAPTER THIRTEEN
KoKo

I pulled my phone from my ear and frowned at it in confusion. "Have you lost your ever-loving mind, Desi?!" I shouted. "Man, fuck that nigga! Change the locks on his bitch ass!"

"I just need someone to watch the kids for me. Ivonka's not picking up her phone. I'll take Delilah with me."

"Are you serious right now?" I asked.

Pierre poked his head out from the walk-in closet. "*Desiree?*" He mouthed.

I nodded.

Desi sniffed. "Girl, I'm so tired of this shit. I'm ready to just move back home with my mom."

"With rowdy five boys? Your mom has a one-bedroom apartment, did you forget?" I reminded.

Pierre poked his head out the closet again and his locs shook violently as he mouthed the word NO repeatedly.

I muted the phone. "Chill out, I wasn't about to ask them to move in. You know her ass ain't leavin' that sorry ass nigga." I said, unmuting the phone.

"So, will you be able to watch them, please?"

"I'm so sorry, Des, but Pierre and I already made plans in advance for tonight."

Pierre held up two thumbs.

KOKO

I whispered into the phone, "Girl, he's been bitchin' about us not spending enough quality time together and I don't feel like hearing his mouth, so I can't cancel. I'm sorry."

"It's okay, I understand. Well. Just call me when you guys get back. Maybe I can drop the kids off later?" She suggested hopefully.

"Desi, it's already nine o'clock. By the time we get home, it'll be after midnight." I stated incredulously.

"You're right." She agreed. "I'll call you tomorrow then."

"What did Desiree want?" Pierre inquired immediately after watching me end the call.

I shook my head. "She wanted to drop the kids off so she could go look for that trifling ass nigga."

"Lucas?"

I rolled my eyes. "Who else? Supposedly, he found himself a new side bitch on top of the other four hundred side bitches he got."

"A new recruit?" Pierre joked.

I nodded. "Yep. What do you think, baby? The diamond studs or the gold hoops?" I held one in each hand up to my ear, as I faced our mirror.

Neither seemed to coordinate with the olive-green Moschino strapless halter dress I was wearing. The dress was form fitting and stopped right above my knees. I had decided to wear my hair the way Pierre liked: slicked back in a simple perfect bun. He called it the ballerina bun.

Pierre walked up to me in a brand new forest green Gucci denim set I had picked out for him earlier that evening. He cocked his head to the side as

I stroked his hairless chin. "I don't know, babe. You look gorgeous to me either way."

He lifted my chin with his index finger and planted a soft kiss on my plum-painted lips. "You don't ever have to worry about me fooling around on you."

"I know, baby." I acknowledged. I placed the gold hoops back in my jewelry box and attached the diamond studs to my ear.

Pierre waited until I was finished, then pulled me closer to him. He began planting kisses all over my neck. "You smell so good, I could eat you up right now. Got me coo-coo for KoKo over here." He joked, but the bulge in his pants confirmed.

"Wanna stay home?" The fact that Pierre was so turned on, aroused me. It had been a long time since he had been this touchy-feely.

"No, we're going to see the play. I had to pull a lot of strings to get these last-minute tickets." He kissed the side of my neck again. "You're the best thing that ever happened to me, Koreen. I want you to know that. Once we walk down that aisle and say 'I do', there is no turning back. I don't believe in divorce. My parents never divorced and neither are we."

"Babe, where is this coming from?" I asked uneasily.

"Nowhere. Just hearing how stressed out Desiree is over her husband made me realize just how lucky we are to have found each other. We're good together, don't you agree?"

"Mmhmm." I nodded.

KOKO

***

I don't know why Pierre had to "pull strings" for us to see *Lawd, I Need a Man*. For one, the theater was barely full, and two, I was Koreen "KoKo"-fuckin' Wilson. I wasn't a gotdamn Kardashian, but my name still carried weight in my hometown. He should've easily been able to score complimentary tickets. Either way, I was ready to go by the first intermission. The play was just that fucking boring.

"Want anything to drink?" Pierre asked during the second intermission. "Popcorn, candy, bottled water, wine?"

What I really needed was a cigarette, but of course Pierre didn't know that. "Get me the strongest alcoholic beverage you can find."

Pierre got up and headed toward the middle aisle. As he made his way out the door, Biggz was heading in the opposite direction, towards the front by the stage.

Shit, he even had better seats than I did, and he wasn't even famous.

I watched Biggz as he stopped at the second row. The patrons seated squirmed as Biggz tried to squeeze his 350-pound frame past them to reach his seat. He knew he was fat as fuck. Why hadn't he just purchased aisle seats?

"What the fuck is this?" My hand flew to my mouth in shock as I continued surveying Biggz.

"What happened? Did I miss something?" I hadn't realized Pierre had returned.

"That was fast."

"I forgot my wallet. It's in your purse remember?"

"It's a clutch." I corrected.

"Okay, your *clutch* then."

I opened my clutch and pulled out his wallet.

"You know what? I gotta use the ladies' room. I'll walk out there with you." I said, handing him his wallet.

"I thought you hated public restrooms."

"I do, but I can't hold it."

There was a line in front of the ladies' room but I didn't give a fuck. I strutted to the front of the line just as an older black woman was coming out.

"Hey, there's a line!" Someone in line protested, causing the other bitter bitches to grumble as well. I didn't care. I needed to make a call. I quickly walked in, shutting the door square in the face of the next bitch in line.

"Where you at?" I got straight to the point as soon as Biggz picked up his phone.

"Out. Where you-?"

"With who?" I cut him off.

"Yo, why you calling me questioning me like I'm a defendant on a witness stand?" He let out a hearty laugh.

Wasn't shit funny to me.

"*Who is that?*" I heard a woman's voice ask in the background.

"You know what, Biggz? *Fuck you, nigga!*" I ended the call before he could lie.

As soon as we had arrived home from the theater, I tried to feed Pierre some bullshit lie so I could leave the house. I had to resolve some unfinished business with Biggz *tonight*.

KOKO

"I need to go check on Desiree, babe. She been texting me all night. I'm worried."

Pierre ceased unbuttoning his long-sleeved shirt and looked up at the ceiling in annoyance. "It's damn near 2 o'clock in the morning. Why do you have to go over there? Just call her."

"I tried callin'. She's not answering."

"Of course she's not. She's probably asleep by now. It's late. You can check on her tomorrow." He suggested.

"You can't tell me what to do. If I wanna leave to check on my girl, then that's exactly what I'm gonna do. I'm not about to ignore my intuition."

"Alright. I'll go with you."

Oh, God. I wanted Pierre's ass to stay home and go to sleep, but I couldn't back out now or he'd be suspicious.

Ugh. "Alright, fine. Let's go."

CHAPTER FOURTEEN
Ivonne

"And he's the reason why you haven't invited me over yet?" Adrian asked.

I nodded sheepishly.

"Well, he's got to go."

I snapped my head up from his blue satin pillow. "What?"

"It's either me or him, babe."

I couldn't tell if he was bluffing and I wasn't about to find out. "He's my best friend."

"You don't need a dude as a best friend. I'm your best friend now, Ivonka. Didn't we agree that your spouse should not only be your lover but also your lifelong best friend?"

I laid my head back on the pillow and took in a deep breath. *Shit.*

"I'm not saying you gotta throw him out on the curb tonight. Just start by giving him notice. Where does this guy work again?" He asked.

I didn't like the way he made it seem as if Isaac was just some random guy off the street. I felt pained at the thought of kicking my oldest friend out after I had insisted that he stay with me.

"Walmart."

"*Psshhh.* Dude wasn't ever planning on leaving."

"I have six bedrooms. That's more than enough space."

Adrian looked over at me in surprise. "You have *six* bedrooms?"

I nodded, hoping that he was now understanding that it really wasn't an issue.

"What type of work you do again?"

I laughed. "I'm an attorney."

Just as I was about to add that I was also living off of a hefty inheritance, he leaned forward to kiss me.

"Mmmn," I purred. "What was that for?"

"Nothing. Just can't wait to start a family with you one day. I know you'll make a terrific mother."

I beamed. I knew then what I had to do. I only hoped that Isaac would understand. I just couldn't lose Adrian or the future that was in store for us.

My thoughts were interrupted by a loud knock on his bedroom door.

Instead of waiting for a response, Doneisha, Adrian's seventeen-year-old daughter opened the door.

"Good morning, baby." Adrian greeted.

"Morning." She greeted dryly as she stood at the door, completely ignoring my existence as she always did. I reminded myself that I would only have to deal with her for a few more months, then she'd be off to Florida State University.

"I need to borrow your car."

"For?" Adrian asked.

She huffed. "To go to Val's." She answered.

That was another thing I didn't understand. As much as Adrian regarded and demanded respect, he allowed his daughter to refer to him and his ex-wife by their first names.

"Why can't your mother pick you up?" He inquired.

"She said she couldn't."

"Probably too busy bumping pussies with another woman." He mumbled irritably.

"Can I just get the car keys, please?"

"Look on top of the refrigerator. How long will you be out?"

"I don't know, ask Val." Doneisha replied before slamming the door shut.

Adrian sighed. "I've been thinking about surprising her with a car as a graduation gift. What you think?"

"You know I support any decision you make."

"And I appreciate you for that. You're a good woman for me."

***

"When was the last time you spoke to Desiree?" KoKo asked the following morning. The tone of her voice revealed that she was genuinely concerned.

"Umm, last time I spoke to her was about three weeks ago when we were all at her house. Why, what's up?"

KoKo had dropped by unexpectedly at 8:30 in the morning, which wasn't a problem except that I was waiting on Adrian to arrive. He and I were supposed to be visiting a couple of car dealerships for Doneisha.

I poured out a cup of coffee for KoKo as I waited for her response.

"I don't know, man. She's just been so distant. Last night Pierre and I stopped by her house to check on her and she wasn't there."

"So?" I asked, shrugging. I walked over to where she sat and placed our mugs on the dining room table.

"It was damn near 3 o'clock in the morning!"

I scrunched my nose. "Why were you and Pierre visiting her at three in the morning? She was probably asleep."

"No. Her car was gone, Vonne. Gone."

"Are you sure? I'm pretty sure she wouldn't just leave with Delilah like that. You should've just called her the next morning. Did you ask her?"

KoKo slammed her hand on the table. "That's what I'm trying to tell you. I haven't been able to reach her. She's been sending me to voicemail and she's never home. *Ever.*"

"Really?" I asked. I couldn't help feeling a little guilty. My world had been so wrapped up in Adrian lately, that I hadn't had a chance to even speak to Desi for the past couple of weeks.

"You haven't seen or spoken to her?" She asked again. This time I could hear a hint of desperation in her voice. "I'm just trying to see if I pissed her off or somethin'."

"She does have a lot on her plate. She probably went to her mother's for a while. Lord knows she need the help."

"You know what? She did mention moving back in with her mother the last time we spoke." KoKo revealed, looking only slightly relieved.

"See?"

"I need your phone, where is it?" She asked.

"It's over here." I retrieved my phone from out my bra.

"Don't put your phone there. It'll give you cancer." She warned, grabbing my phone from my hand.

"Wait, I'm waiting on a phone call."

She began punching numbers on my cell phone, then held the phone up to her ear.

"Calling Desi?"

She nodded.

"*Shit*." She said. "Fuckin' voicemail again." She handed me back my phone.

"How about we drop by her mother's when I get back? I'll come pick you up so we can ride together."

"What time? I have plans with Moet."

I raised an eyebrow. "But I thought--"

KoKo shook her head. "Nope. Miraculously my bottle of pills haven't been disappearing anymore. Plus, my bae just separated from that sorry ass husband of hers. He can't keep a job to save his life."

I gave KoKo a quizzical look. "You've been asking that woman to leave her husband and you're on the brink of entering a marriage. Does that make any sense to you?"

She shrugged. "She cool with it. I don't know why you so bothered."

"I don't even know why I asked. I'll text you when I'm done running my errands and we'll figure out a meeting time."

"Did you catch Mindy Mathers show last night?" She asked.

I crinkled my nose. "You know I don't watch that trash."

"Neither do I. I stopped watching that bitch years ago but Biggz happened to catch her show last night. He text me to ask about my ass injections."

"Why?" I asked, unable to put the pieces together.

"He said that Mindy reported that somebody from my 'camp' leaked info that confirms that I had my ass done. He wanted to know if it was true."

"What did you say?" I asked curiously.

KoKo looked at me as if I were stupid. "I said no. I'm taking that to my grave."

"What information did Mindy say they have on you?" I asked.

She shrugged indifferently. "I don't know. I didn't care enough to ask but I wonder if that's why Desi's avoiding me."

"You think she told?" I laughed. "Why would she leak that? She's had a boob job from the same doctor. Why would she anyway? It doesn't make sense, KoKo. Think about it."

"You're probably right. Well if she calls, let her know I been looking for her. I gotta run." She picked up what looked like a blue alligator Hermès handbag.

"Wait, is that Hermès?" I asked, completely dumbfounded.

She glanced down at her purse proudly. "Well it's damn sure not a knock-off."

"That's a *seventy*-thousand-dollar handbag, KoKo."

"I would think I know how much this bag set me back." She looked insulted.

"You bought that?"

She scrunched up her face. "Of course, I bought it. I love gator skin."

I was hoping my expression didn't show how taken back I was. I didn't think Koreen was making that type of money on a video vixen's salary.

"Surprise Pierre didn't have a bitch-fit over it. Isn't he a vegan?" I asked.

"Pierre don't know and Pierre don't need to know."

"But don't you guys have a wedding to-"

"*Oh. My.God!*" KoKo and I both jumped at the sound of Isaac's voice. He held his right hand up to his mouth in a fist.

KoKo smiled warmly, as she walked over to him. "You must be Isaac." She held out her hand.

"Yes, yes." Isaac stammered. "I'm *Koreen the Dream*. Wait, no, no. Isaac! I'm Isaac!"

KoKo giggled in amusement as Isaac shook her hand.

CHAPTER FIFTEEN
KoKo

"Can I get my hand back, please?" I smiled.

Isaac wasn't as bad on the eyes as I'd originally thought he would be. He was really short with locs longer than Pierre's. His facial hair was so unkempt, he resembled a mountain man. His wardrobe could definitely use a major makeover. His flannel shirt and denim shorts did not match and were ridiculously wrinkled. I was sure that with a clean-shaven face and updated garments, Ivonka would defintiely give him some play.

"Oh-uh- sorry about that." He released my hand from his grip. "Do you mind taking a picture with me?"

Ivonne interjected. "No, Isaac. Not today. We're heading out."

Isaac snapped his fingers as if remembering something. "I think Adrian's outside."

"He's been outside all this time? Why didn't you invite him in?"

Isaac shrugged, then exited the kitchen.

I clapped excitedly. "Yes! I finally get to meet Adrian!"

Ivonne moved her index finger from side to side.

"Not today, Koreen. Next time." She said firmly.

She scrunched up her face. "Why? It's only gonna take a second."

"Absolutely not. Next time."

"He must be ugly."

"He is *not* ugly."

"Who?" Ivonne and I both turned towards the direction of the voice.

Isaac and an older gentleman had walked in. He had to be Adrian. Because of his curly graying hair, I wasn't quite sure if he was black, Hispanic or Native American. He skin-tone was a bright caramel color and he looked to be in his mid to late fifties, which wasn't much of a surprise because Ivonka loved her some geriatric penis. His full beard and grungy clothes gave him a gruff rugged look.

Ivonne rushed towards the man and he embraced her with open arms. If I didn't know better, I thought I seen Isaac roll his eyes before walking off.

"Adrian, this is Koreen. She's one of my good friends. Koreen, meet Adrian." She introduced us.

Adrian took a step forward to shake my hand. "Nice to meet you. I feel like I know you from somewhere." He squinted as we shook hands.

"Yeah, babe. You might've seen her in a couple of music videos and magazine covers." Ivonne informed.

"And movies." I added. Granted, the parts I had were small roles, but I was still an actress nonetheless. "You can call me KoKo."

He looked surprise. "You're *KoKo*? The official ambassador for beautiful chocolate women everywhere. My daughter loves you! Every other week she's asking for money to do her hair like KoKo's or get an outfit like KoKo's. You have amazing skin. Do you mind taking a picture with me so I can send it to her? It would sure make her day."

I smiled, enjoying the attention. "Sure."

Ivonne smiled, resembling a Cheshire cat. "Great! While you're doing that, I'm gonna grab my keys real quick. Then we can head out."

This was the reason why it was my number one rule to *never* leave my house half-steppin'. Pierre didn't get it. He didn't see why I took over an hour to get ready. Even if it was only to grab the mail. Today I was dressed much more casual than usual but I was still cute. I had slipped on one of my lavender velour sweat suits and made sure that my waist-length curls had been curled to perfection.

"Do you mind if I ask for a hug? I'm so sorry, I hope I don't sound too forward. I'm just a lil star struck. I'm from a small town in Mississippi and I've never actually met a real-life celebrity before." He rambled.

I was flattered and I also completely understood. It wasn't my first time having that effect on a fan. I wasn't too keen on hugging a random stranger, though. Since he was one of my best friend's man, I decided to just suck it up.

"Sure, no problem." I nodded, intending to make it as quick as possible. He leaned in and held me in a tight embrace. I felt his lips pressed down the side of my neck while his hands travelled south. Before I knew what was happening, he grabbed a handful of both my ass cheeks in both palms.

"The fuck off of me!" I whispered. I shoved him with as much force as possible just as Isaac entered the kitchen.

Isaac stopped mid-stroll and furrowed his brow.

"Got em!" The sound of Ivonne's heels striking the marble floors quickly made their way back towards the kitchen.

"What just happened?" Isaac asked, looking from me to Adrian.

"I got my keys, babe. Ready?" Ivonne asked Adrian.

I was so angry I couldn't speak. Instead, I held on to my handbag and stormed off.

"What's wrong?" I heard Ivonne ask.

***

"I need a fuckin' cigarette." I laid my head against the seat of my Rolls-Royce.

I also needed a friend to talk to. I had called Desi as soon as I had jumped in my Rover and the bitch sent me to voicemail again. Talking to Pierre was out of the question. He would swear that I was overreacting.

"Yo, what's good?" Biggz asked, peeping the angry expression on my face. "Don't be comin' in here with the bullshit, KoKo." Biggz said. He tried to kiss me at door, but instead I brushed past him.

"Fuck you." I spat.

"When?" He teased, following me to his master bedroom.

"Who were you with last night?" I asked.

KOKO

"Here we go." He lit a blunt, plopped his heavy frame on the bed, then grabbed the remote control to turn the television on.

I hastily walked over to his side of the bed and slapped the fucking remote out of his hand with as much force as I could possibly muster. The back of the controller sprang open as the remote hit the floor.

"I seen you with that bitch."

"What bitch? Where?"

"You wanna play dumb?!" I shouted irrationally.

Biggz put out his blunt before lifting up from the bed. He grabbed my arms forcefully. "KoKo, what the fuck do you want? Do your dumb ass even know what the fuck it is that you want?"

"Fuck you, Malik!" I spat.

He chuckled, releasing my arms. "Government name, hunh? Alright, *Koreen*. Just let me know when. I'll fuck the shit outta you."

"Fuck both of y'all. She's just using your dumb ass. I hope you know that." I said, heading towards the bedroom door.

Biggz grabbed my arm, forcing me to halt in my tracks. "You introduced us, remember? I didn't ask for no fuckin' threesome, you wanted that shit, remember?"

I rolled my eyes, knowing he was right. I didn't understand why the fuck I was so angry at Biggz. I should've been cussin' Moet's triflin' ass out right this second but I knew I couldn't. It wasn't like her and I were in a relationship, but she knew I was really feeling her. I think I was upset at Biggz for messing with my girl behind my back. The whole thing just seemed sneaky.

I had no cigarettes and I needed some release. It was only 10 in the morning and already it was turning out to be a stressful day.

"Come fuck me, baby." I removed my jogging suit and undergarments, letting them fall to the floor, then laid spread eagle on his California king-sized bed.

Biggz stood at the foot of the bed, looking uneasy. "You didn't even want me kissing you a minute ago. Now you wanna fuck?"

"Yes, daddy. Come 'ere." I purred seductively.

"I can't. I was on my way out when you came in. I gotta be somewhere."

"Where?"

"Here we go with the twenty-one questions."

I sat up. "Alright, fine. I'll just stay here while you're out." I suggested. It wasn't like I wasn't used to doing that anyway.

"Why?" He asked. He glanced at his watch, then back at me.

This set me off. "What the fuck is the problem? It's not like I don't have a fucking key! Are you meeting up with the bitch again?!" I shouted, crawling on my knees to where he stood at the foot of the bed. I pushed my palms against his heavy frame as hard as I could. Then, for whatever reason, I burst into tears. I wasn't even sure why I was crying.

That was a lie. I knew why.

Biggz grabbed both my wrists, then sat on the bed besides me. Whatever it was that was bothering me, I released through the tears as I buried my face in his chest. He didn't say anything. He rubbed my back and continued doing so until I stopped weeping.

"I'll cancel, alright?" He said quietly.

I was slightly embarrassed, yet I still managed to nod.

I could hear him tapping away on his iPhone.

"What the fuck is really going on, bae?" He asked softly.

"I'm pregnant... I think. I took two tests this morning. Both said the same thing." I confessed with my head still buried in his chest.

"Hunh?" He grabbed my shoulders and pulled me away from him. I looked up to see his eyes bulging wide open.

"Nigga, I'm pregnant. I don't know how the fuck this happened." Warm tears were now trailing down my cheeks.

He smiled. "Oh, shit. I'm finally gonna be a father. I hope it's a boy. I always wanted a junior."

I punched him in the chest. He released me to grab his chest.

"I'm getting married in a year. I can't walk down the aisle pregnant!"

"It takes less than a year to deliver a baby. You'll have my baby by then."

"I don't even fucking know if it's yours!" I sobbed again, burying my face in my palms.

"We can take a DNA test when the baby gets here. Don't worry, boo. This is a blessing in disguise, babe."

I sobbed harder.

"KoKo, stop." He said, trying to pry my hands away from my face

"Koreen, look at me. Please." He pleaded softly.

I looked up. "I'm sorry, Biggz but I don't want this baby and it's not like I can just get rid of it. At least not without leaving the country. I don't need this shit leaking to the press." I explained through tears.

Biggz took in a deep breath, then gave me a serious look. "You're having my baby, KoKo. This is my blessing."

"It might not even be yours, Biggz. Do you not understand that?" I desperately wanted it to be Pierre's. He had just spoken about how he wanted us to try for a son as soon as we were married.

"Well, there's a fifty-fifty chance and I'm willing to pay for all of your maternity expenses until we find out. You won't have to pay back a dime if it ends up being his." He said earnestly.

I wanted to tell him that it wasn't a fifty-fifty chance. Within two months I had fucked Pierre, Biggz, Ganja Green, *and* Bernard.

CHAPTER SIXTEEN
Ivonne

"So, KoKo might be pregnant." I revealed. Then quickly added, "But please don't tell anyone. She would kill me if she knew I told anyone."

Adrian took my hand into his across the intimate candlelit table. "Baby, I'm your best friend now. Your secrets are safe with me. I won't tell a soul."

Adrian suggested we have dinner that night at a 5-star restaurant, so we were waiting on our server to arrive with our cuisine when I brought up KoKo.

"I'm serious. The media is always looking for a reason to drag her through the mud. I need you to keep this between us, please." I urged.

He nodded. "I got you."

"Alright." I relaxed a bit, then continued. "She doesn't know who the father is, either. It might even be her ex-husband's." I said, shaking my head.

"Woooord? She still fuckin' with his ass? I thought he was gay!" He whispered.

"I know. Believe me, I'm just as surprise."

"She keeping it?" He asked.

I shrugged. "I have no clue." I answered, taking a sip of my Dom Perignon.

Adrian shook his head. "Word around Miami is she's an ex-stripper who charged $20 for blow jobs in an alley behind the club. Ain't no tellin' who her baby's father is."

My drink spewed out my mouth, as I held my chest in a fit of laughter. "She has *never* stripped. *Never*. Trust me. That was just a rumor. People tend to think all video vixens were former strippers or hos anyway."

"You sure about that?" He asked.

"She's never stripped." I repeated adamantly.

"I meant the part about her bein' a thot."

"You know what? I don't feel comfortable continuing this discussion." I said, glancing around the dimly lit establishment.

"Hey, you brought her up, not me." He chuckled.

"But I do have a question for you." He asked before taking a sip of his Trump Premium Vodka.

"What is it?"

"Did she say anything to you about why she left the way she did the other day?" He eyed me curiously.

I shook my head. "No. When I called her later that night to ask, she said it could wait. Then she brought up the whole pregnancy fiasco."

"I think I know why, but I don't need you running back and tell her what I said." He said.

"Oh? Tell me. What happened? Isaac said she seemed pretty upset right before I had walked in, but he didn't know what was wrong either."

Adrian exhaled and my stomach formed knots. I had a feeling I wasn't gonna like whatever he had to say.

KOKO

"She tried to give me her number. I don't think she's the type of woman that handles rejection well."

"She did *what*?" I asked, raising both brows.

Adrian looked down at his drink as he continued, "She tried to pass me a business card or something with her personal line scribbled on it. She said we didn't have to tell you. May God strike me if I'm lying."

"*Koreen* said that?" I asked again.

"Yes, woman. *Koreen. Koreen the Dream.* I didn't wanna upset you. It was probably nothing. Maybe she was high. I read somewhere that she's addicted to painkillers or heroin or some shit." He was speaking about her as if we were talking about someone I barely knew. I didn't think KoKo would intentionally go after my man. She would never do anything like that. Would she?

Adrian continued. "But when you brought up the whole pregnancy thing and her not knowing who knocked her up..." His voice trailed off as he shook his head. "That bitch is a slut. You don't need that type of friend."

I sat there silently and in shock. I tried digesting the information that had just been revealed to me. Sure, KoKo was promiscuous but she had never ever betrayed Desi and I. At least not that I knew of. However, Adrian had no reason to lie to me. He had even admitted to being a fan of hers. What did he possibly have to gain?

"You know what, babe. Let's change the subject. I can see this is upsetting you." Adrian suggested, just as our waiter arrived with our seafood cuisine.

"Monsieur, Madame. Enjoy." Our waiter bowed before departing.

"Mmm this smells good!" Adrian said, licking his lips. "Shall I say grace?"

I bowed my head as he grabbed both my hands and led us into prayer. I beamed inside. This was exactly what I loved about Adrian. Not only was he extremely handsome, but he knew I had always yearned for a God-fearing man. I kept my eye open a few seconds to admire Adrian in a black Ferragamo blazer. The specks of grey in his beard blended in with his soft curly hair, made him even more appealing to me. I closed my eyes just as he was wrapping up his prayer.

"You're a beautiful woman, Ivonka. You know that? I don't care how fat you think you are. You're a gem in my eyes, baby." He said afterwards. He took turns kissing both of my hands before releasing them.

I beamed, shyly.

"You're the best thing that ever happened to me. How'd I get so lucky?" He asked.

"Thank you, Adrian." I blushed. For the first time since losing my father, I felt loved. Worthy. Adrian always had a way of doing that. He knew I struggled with my self-image and self-worth. Yet, he still accepted me for me.

"With that being said, I'd like to make a toast." He raised his glass and I followed suit. "To the woman of my dreams. Never thought I'd ever find you. Thank you for everything you've done for me and Doneisha. You'll make a wonderful wife and mother to our children one day. Cheers to you, lady." We clinked our glasses as I blushed again.

"I'm so happy I found you as well, Adrian. You mean the world to me." I admitted, getting emotional. I dabbed the corner of my eye with a napkin.

"I meant what I said, babe. Doneisha really likes her new car. She'll be in college soon so she'll really need it. I appreciate you paying for the car, you didn't have to do that."

I nodded. He was right. I didn't have to but I had wanted to make a great impression on Adrian. Not to mention it had earned me some brownie points with Doneisha. She had actually started warming up to me once her father mentioned that I had been the one to pay off her Prius in full. The charge had hardly made a dent in my account anyway.

Adrian continued, "I also can't thank you enough for putting down the down payment on my Mercedes."

"You're welcome, babe." I beamed. Charging twenty grand on my charge card for a brand-new Benz had all been Adrian's idea. However, I had no regrets about it. I considered it all an investment towards our future.

Adrian took in a deep breath. "I quit my job at the lab."

My eyes widened in shock. "When? Why? I thought you loved your job and what about your car note, Adrian."

Adrian reached for my hand. "I did love my job. I just think it's time for me to pursue my dreams of becoming an entrepreneur. I thought you of all people would understand. I need my woman, my future wife, to be my biggest cheerleader, investor, and supporter by my side right now."

Thinking about the car I had just leased under my name for him, I sighed. "So, what type of business are we talking about? Do you have a business plan?"

He smiled broadly. "Business plan? Haven't gotten that far yet but my boy Keon and I been thinking about a strip joint slash sports bar slash casino type of establishment."

Something inside me couldn't help feeling uneasy. "What about the car and your rent? Do you have enough in savings to be able to afford the payments for the next year or two? You do know most businesses don't make a strong profit the first couple of years."

"So, I've been meaning to ask you..." He said as he cracked open a lobster tail. "About that big ass mansion you're living in all by your lonesome."

"I'm not always alone." I admitted hesitantly.

"There's always someone there with me. If it's not the housekeeper, then it's the cook, and of course there's Isaac."

"Did you give ol' boy his notice yet?" Adrian asked.

"Yeah, I told him last night."

"What he say about it?"

I shook my head as I poked into a sliced potato with my fork. "He didn't say much. Just said he would be out by the end of the week."

"Didn't I tell you he'd find somewhere to go? That's a grown ass nigga. Now had you not said anything, ain't no telling how long his moochin' ass would've still been living there. You did the right thing, baby girl."

I didn't bother telling Adrian that I had offered to pay a whole year's rent for Isaac's apartment when he found one. Isaac had declined but did take me up on my offer to help with the security deposit and a hotel room for the month. He refused to stay at my place until he found an apartment. In fact, he was livid when I broke the news to him over the phone.

My thoughts continued to wander to Isaac throughout the remainder of our dinner date.

"Did he put you up to this? You've only known this guy, what, two months?" Isaac had inquired last night on the phone.

My silence spoke volumes.

I heard him let out a deep breath. "Just watch out for this guy, Von. Seems like he's trying to isolate you from everyone."

"I understand you're upset--" I started to say.

"Actually, I'm more disappointed than upset."

"Adrian is good for me, Isaac."

"How do you know? You barely know the guy!"

"But I feel like I've known him my whole life. We have a connection."

"Do you realize that you've said the exact same thing about the last three guys you've dated?"

I inhaled uncomfortably. "Isaac, I understand that you are in love with me but--"

He let out a loud cackle, interrupting me. "You know what? Do what the fuck you want. Don't say I didn't warn you. I'll be out by the end of the week." He said, before hanging up on me.

"Baby?" Adrian said, snapping his fingers.

I shook all thoughts of Isaac and KoKo from my thoughts.

"The check." He said, sliding the bill across the table in my direction.

I snapped open my clutch to retrieve my American Express card.

CHAPTER SEVENTEEN
Desi

"*Mierda!* Where the fuck is that gun?!" I shouted in frustration, but there was no reason to shout. I was inside the mansion alone, which was rare.

Lucas had been outside for the last ten minutes trying to convince his little whore to vacate our property. My mom had taken the kids to her apartment as soon as that bitch had pulled up to my house. I was Mrs. Lucas Loren. I was the HBIC. How dare his bitch pull up to our house just as we had arrived home, as if we had been followed. As if she had been watching us while we were out celebrating *my* husband's fifty-first birthday at his favorite Sicilian restaurant. My mother and children had been there. We could have easily all been in danger like the last time, when one of Lucas' crazy ass side chicks tried to attack me at a Whole Foods downtown. Enough was enough. I was tired of these brazen ass side bitches.

I quickly raced to the bathroom and snatched open the door to the medicine cabinet. I hastily grabbed the prescription bottle of Zoloft.

"Shit!" It was empty.

I kicked off my gold Moschino kitten heels, sending each shoe crashing against the wall and dug my feet into a pair of blue Jordans. I didn't bother changing out of my long red sequined Alexander

McQueen dress with the high splits on each side, my husband's favorite. The one he had bought a year ago and had often referred to it as the Jessica Rabbit dress. To top it off, I had spent 2 hours flat ironing my long red rebellious curls and had styled it similar to the cartoon vixen just to please my beloved husband.

I found a purple semi-automatic handgun that Lucas must've tucked away in an old locked drawer. I snatched an old Glock in the same drawer and decided that I could use both. With my adrenaline still pumping, I jogged back outside in my red sequined dress.

Lucas was standing opposite of the young Venezuelan homewrecker, who looked no older than twenty. He pleaded with her to leave. "Paola, we can talk about this later." Lucas begged, his back facing me.

The young woman, dressed from head-to-toe in a black designer baby doll dress, donning a head full of dark flowing hair, stood by the driver's side door of her silver Lexus. I'd noticed long ago that they were always brunette. I had been his first red head, so he said.

Her door was wide open as she stood halfway in between the door frame.

"I'm having this baby and you're gonna take care of it, Lucas! Even if I have to put your old ass on child support!" She shouted in Spanish.

Enough was enough. I shot a bullet straight in the air with the purple semi-automatic, startling both Lucas and the Venezuelan bitch.

"*Aye dios!* Desi!" Lucas shouted, crouching. "Put that shit away before the neighbors call 9-1-1!" He warned in Spanish, but my mind was too far gone. I had zero fucks left to give.

I aimed the Glock towards Lucas.

Still crouched, Lucas raised both hands in front of his chest. "Put the gun down, Desi." He enunciated each word slowly in Spanish.

From out the corner of my eye I noticed Lucas' whore jumping back in her Lexus. With the Glock still aimed at Lucas, I pointed the other gun, the purple one, at her front passenger side tire and pulled the trigger twice. The bullets tore through the rubber and air quickly rushed out.

"*Aye dios mio!*" She cried out.

Charging towards the silver Lexus, I aimed the handgun at the bitch through her front passenger-side window.

"Where the fuck you think you goin'?!" I shouted.

I could hear Lucas on the floor behind me. "*Por favor*, Desi-"

With the Glock still pointed down at Lucas, I pulled the trigger and the bullet grazed his earlobe. Paola cried out in horror. My husband held his ear and released some expletives in Spanish.

"I promise, next time I *won't* miss." I threatened him.

I turned my attention back to my husband's whore. His latest mistress. The Venezuelan homewrecker who just couldn't leave my family the fuck alone.

I cocked the gun.

The young feisty Venezuelan bitch full of attitude, that had pulled up to my house half an hour ago to raise hell was replaced with a blubbering snotty sniveling mess. Tears were flowing freely as she whimpered, "*Por favooor! I have twins at home. Please don't shoot me!*"

"Oh really?" I retorted. "Well I have *six* children and you sure didn't give a shit when you were fucking their father, so why should I give a shit about your kids, bitch?"

"*Pleeeaase*, don't shoot." Her blubbering was annoying the fuck outta me.

I continued. "Then you have the nerve to bring your old ass Lexus to my house," I could feel myself getting angrier. "Following my family around. *Hijo de puta!* I'm tired of you disrespectful bitches!" I shouted, now aiming both guns towards her dome.

"You come to my house talking some nonsense about a fucking pregnancy! I oughta kill yo ass and that bastard-baby right now! Bitch, is you crazy?! Hunh? Are you?! *Answer me, you whore!*"

The stupid Venezuelan bitch began crying hysterically.

"No, Please! I'll get rid of it. *Lo siento!* I'm sorry!"

The dumb bitch was trying to shield her pathetic snot-covered face with her arms. As if her arms were bullet-proof.

I cackled. "Should've thought about that before you laid down with my husband, bitch."

Ignoring her whimpers, I squeezed both triggers.

CHAPTER EIGHTEEN
Ivonne

"Wanna hear something really crazy?" I asked KoKo from behind my mahogany desk.

She grabbed the contract I had just reviewed from my grasp, and carefully placed it inside a red leather portfolio.

"Okay, what is it?" She answered cheerfully, happy that I had given the contract for her reality show a thumbs-up.

I had never had the chance to confront her about what Adrian had revealed to me. I'd like to think that KoKo was better than that, but my doubts had been eating away at me.

"Adrian thinks Des may have been the culprit behind your missing pills." I informed.

KoKo rolled her eyes as she sucked her teeth. "What the fuck does he know? He don't even know us like that."

I gave her a weak smile. "Well, I've told him a lot about you guys. I told you it was crazy."

KoKo shot me a blank look. "Why in the world are you discussin' me and Desiree with this man?"

I was genuinely shocked that KoKo was snapping at me this way. I was sure Pierre knew some personal things about Desi and I. That was to be expected when you were in a relationship.

"It's not like that, KoKo." I tried reassuring her. "I don't tell him everything."

KoKo tucked her red leather portfolio under her armpit. "Well do me this favor and keep my name out your mouth when you speaking to that nigga."

My eyes widened in surprise. I chuckled nervously. "You are really overreacting, girl. We barely mention you."

"You laughin'. I'm serious. Do *not* tell that nigga any of my business, Ivonne."

I held my hands up in front of me in defeat. "Alright, alright. I won't tell him anything about you."

"You ain't tell him I was pregnant, did you?"

I shook my head no. I immediately felt awful for lying.

Satisfied with my response, KoKo used both her palms to smooth out her gold Dior skirt before placing her portfolio back on her lap. "To tell you the truth, I've kinda had my suspicions."

I leaned forward. "About Adrian?"

She gave me an exasperated look. "About Des. I suspected it was her when my shit stopped disappearing even after Moet and I had started fuckin' around again."

"You still seeing Moet? I thought-"

KoKo interrupted. "That was before I stopped fucking with the backstabbing bitch."

I was still confused. If KoKo wasn't in a relationship with Moet or Biggz, how could either of them have betrayed her?

KoKo continued. "I think that's why the bitch been avoiding us."

"Who?"

"*Desiree!*" KoKo huffed. "I don't care about that shit though. She should've just asked if she really wanted them. I would've gotten her the hook-up."

I shook my head in disbelief. "I knew Desi was unhappy. I just didn't think it was to this extent."

"Not everyone who pop pills got problems." KoKo stated.

"I'm just saying. I would have never fathomed that she was an addict."

KoKo interjected. "No one said anything about her being an addict."

"Adrian thinks so."

"How would he know? He's never met her." She snarled.

I ignored her comment and glanced at my watch. "How about we go grab some lunch? Didn't you just land an endorsement with Melanin Cosmetics?" I asked. "We should be out having a celebratory lunch, girl!"

Her eyes lit up. "Yesss, girl. My first real endorsement!"

"That's not true. You had a deal with that rapper, I forgot her name, but you know who I'm talking about. She hired you as her spokesmodel for her line of waist trainers, remember?"

"That bitch, Stormy Knight."

I snapped my fingers. "Right! Stormy. She was legit, too."

"Girl that was waaay back from when I was still married to Bernard. Her ass dropped me as soon as I had gained weight after my divorce. Fuck her. I've been thinkin about starting my own lingerie line." She revealed with bright eyes.

"That would definitely take off for you. You have the best body to pull off the lingerie line." I admitted.

KoKo smiled as she stood up and struck a pose. "I sure do. Thanks to my baby. He help keep this body on point, honey."

I couldn't help eyeing the butt injections that she had purchased years ago, much to Pierre's chagrin. The same injections she often denied to her critics about having.

"Well, congratulations on your new endorsement. We definitely need to celebrate with lunch and then dinner this weekend. I'll try to reach Desiree."

"What time is it?" She asked.

I glanced at the time on my computer. "It's 1."

"I have a couple of hours to burn before meeting up with Bernie so it's cool."

I raised both brows.

"It was a one-time thing. I bumped into him at Ganja's album release party a couple of months ago." She explained before I could even ask.

"Wait, he knows Ganja Green?" I asked incredulously. I couldn't wait to tell Adrian about this new revelation.

She nodded unashamedly. "Their families are both from the same place in Jamaica. Anyway," KoKo continued, "I ran into him at the party. We were both faded. One thing led to another, and next thing I know, I'm at his studio apartment getting my back blown out."

"*Whaaaat?*"

KoKo smiled. "And it was *good*. I hadn't realized how much I missed Bernie's dick until it was in me." She smirked.

"You're going to hell." I said.

"With designer gasoline drawers on." She added.

"So you two planning on getting back together?"

"*Girl bye*, I don't fuck around with bisexual dudes."

Apparently, you do, is what I wanted to say but didn't have the balls to.

"I'm just meeting up with him to let him know in person that it was all just a mistake."

I gave her a skeptical look.

"He doesn't have my number. We've been emailing back and forth but I'm about to be doing this reality show soon. I don't need no scandal, no drama, no nothin' coming up while we're shooting this reality show. Pierre would kill me. I'll be damned if I'm left at the altar on national T.V."

"I think I understand where you're coming from." I sympathized.

"I'm getting hungry. You still got that chef over at your crib?"

"Stefan? Yes."

"Let's have lunch at your place. I don't feel like dealing with the razzi today." She said, referring to the paparazzi.

"That's fine." I agreed, gathering my handbag and briefcase. "I was planning on finishing up the remainder of my work at home anyway. Oh, wait." I said, remembering something.

"What?" KoKo asked, rising to her feet.

"I forgot to tell you: Adrian moved in about a week ago."

KoKo's eyes bulged. "Wait a minute. Did his ass get evicted or somethin? Why the damn rush?"

I laughed. "There is no rush and no, he didn't get evicted. He's achemist. He makes decent money." I lied.

After announcing that he had quit his job, I ended up having to make the payments on his new Mercedes that I had purchased. It turned out Adrian didn't have a penny saved. I allowed him and Doneisha to move in. Her being there wasn't that bad. Most of the time she stayed with her mother and would be dorming at FSU in a couple of months.

"This is crazy." KoKo said, sitting back down. "He cool with what's-his-face under the same roof? I didn't think they liked each other."

"Isaac moved out a couple of weeks ago." I revealed.

"Woooord? That man relocated from Baton Rouge just to be with you, not knowing a soul down here and....wow." She shook her head.

"What?" I asked.

"He told you to give Isaac the boot, didn't he?" She asked.

"What would make you say that?"

She shook her head again, this time with a disgusted look on her face. "You're such a 'Pick-Me'."

I crinkled my brows. "A what?"

"You heard me. A *'Pick-Me'* chick. Your whole existence centers around finding 'Mr. Right'. Do and say anything and everything to be accepted or approved by a man in hopes of being his chosen one. Basically, a desperate bitch. Girl fuck these niggas. Get a mind of your own. You need to start doing you, boo. Life does not end if you're single, chile."

"I am not a pick-me." I protested.

"Only a pick-me would accept a so-called *picnic* in a nigga car as a date." She said with a look of disgust.

I rolled my eyes. "That happened one time and that was years ago."

"You were still old enough to know better." She snapped.

"I'm just not like other females who need a man to spend a lot of money on a first date. I don't mind hanging out in the backyard stargazing, eating at a fast food joint, or watching movies with him at his house on a first date. So what? I'm not that hard to please. I have my own money. Sorry if I'm not materialistic."

Both of KoKo's eyes widened dramatically. "Bitch, that's the fuckin' problem! No standards. You happy with just the bare minimum. No chase. Settle for any man who throw you a little attention. You even stopped wearing weaves when you read comments from men on Facebook claiming they loved natural-haired sistas."

"That's a boldface lie. My hairstylist suggested I give weaves a break." I lied. "And as far as my so-called low standards, not every woman believes there's a need to be so high-maintenance. Excuse me for not sleeping with a man in exchange for a pocketbook. I'm sorry that I have my own money and don't need a man to take care of me."

KoKo took a step forward. Her large dark brown eyes glared into mine. "Number one, I don't need a man to take care of me. I make my own money. Shit, as a matter of fact, I happen to be the breadwinner at my house-"

"And that may be why you don't respect Pierre." I blurted out and instantly regretted it.

"Keep my fiancé's name out ya mouth." She growled through clenched teeth. "You're the last person I need giving commentary about my relationship. You the reason why Desi stayed with that nigga the last time she was ready to serve him with divorce papers."

I placed a hand on my chest in amazement. "I'm the reason?"

KoKo pointed an index finger towards my chest. "*You*. A year ago, around Mother's Day. We were at our usual spot at *Trendy Indies*. Desi had confided in us about going to see a divorce attorney that your ass recommended her to. She was ready to pack her bags and bounce and you sat there and talked her out of it!"

I said nothing as I briefly reflected on that evening. I was only looking out for her by reminding her that they could always try therapy again. I felt like I had been honest when I told her that becoming a single mom would be a bad look for her. Whether KoKo wanted to accept it or not, she knew very well single black mothers were the most judged and criticized in the black community. Especially one with five children and another on the way. She had no education and no previous work experience. She was living every woman's dream: multimillion dollar house with the picket fence, kids, and a wealthy husband. I understood he often cheated, but that was something that I was sure they could still work out with time. No marriage was perfect. I had even given her suggestions on things that she could do as wife to make him happier and keep him home. She always refused to take my advice. Besides, Desiree was a grown woman. It was ultimately her choice to stay or leave.

"Are you listenin'?" KoKo asked, interrupting my thoughts.

"Yes, I'm listening." I lied.

"*Well*? Are you gonna answer my question?"

I gave her a blank look.

"When was the last time you were single?" She repeated.

I looked at her as if she were dumb. "Right before I met Adrian."

"I meant when was the last time you weren't dating or talking to anybody. Just chilling and doing you? When was the last time you took a break to be with yourself, Ivonne?"

I tried to think.

"See? Honey, you're a serial dater. Your old ass can't stand to be alone. The thought of being by yourself scares you half to death. We all go through that phase but my problem with you is that yo ass too damn old to still be stuck in this cycle."

The muscles in my entire body began to feel tense as anger rose in me. It was my turn to glare at her.

"What is this? *Iyanla: Fix My Life*? Just admit you have a problem with Adrian."

KoKo looked unbothered as she placed a hand on her hip. "You right. I can't stand that nigga. You can do better, Ivonne. That nigga ain't shit."

"Oh? *He's* not shit?"

"Yeah, he ain't shit." She stated, staring me down.

"I guess it would take one to know one." I snapped.

"*Excuse me?*" She looked taken back.

"He told me what you did. That was foul." I stated, shocked that I had finally let the cat out the bag.

KoKo stood up and towered over my desk. "And what did he tell you? I can't wait to hear this shit."

I stood behind my desk and crossed my arms. "He said you tried to give him your number." I finally said, raising a brow.

"And I bet your stupid ass believed that just like the pick-me you are." She shook her head. "You know what? I wasn't gonna say anything because I know your little relationship will be short-lived like the others, but your man came on to me, heiffa. I have a man. What would I need with his blue-pill-poppin' ass? Please, he doesn't even make enough to *look* my way."

I thought about what Adrian said about KoKo charging for blow jobs. "So, the only thing stopping you from fucking my man is his income bracket?"

KoKo sighed in exasperation. "Oh my gawd. I'm so done with this conversation. Forget lunch. I'm going home to my *fiancé* and my *child*." She turned to leave.

She held the office door open, then turned to face

me. "You know what? For someone so educated and with so much book-smarts, you dumb as shit."

CHAPTER NINETEEN
Ivonne

"Who is it?!" Isaac shouted from behind a stained apartment door.

"It's me!" I answered with a grimace, still trying to make out what the brown stains outside his front door were.

"Me, who?"

"Open the damn door, Isaac!"

I leaned towards the door to sniff the brown smudges just as Isaac pulled the door open. He greeted me in his usual black beanie that were holding up his long brown locs. His clothes were disheveled, mismatched, wrinkled.

He gave me an amused look, then glanced at the stains. "Trust me, you don't wanna smell that."

"Enough said." I replied.

I walked past him and entered a small living room. From where I stood I could see his bathroom door and a small kitchen area. I eyed the twin-size bed that seemed totally out of place in a corner of the living room.

"Wow, this is..."

"Tiny?" He answered. "It's called a studio apartment, Ivonka."

I couldn't help crinkling my forehead. "This is a studio apartment?"

"It is." He answered.

I walked across the small living area and opened the bathroom door. At least the bathroom was clean.

"I don't know, I always thought studio apartments were little studios that music producers and musicians rented out for business." I admitted, confused.

"Yeah you definitely need to start crossing the bridge more often, Von." He suggested, referring to the MacArthur Causeway. The infamous bridge that separated South Beach from Downtown Miami. The rich and the poor.

"Have a seat." He pointed at the twin-sized bed. "I didn't see the point of buying a sofa. Not enough space." He informed, looking around.

I felt a pang of guilt as I took a seat on the shabby mattress. He sat next to me. "Want something to drink? I don't have any wine, only have water right now. I wasn't expecting company." He stood up.

"No, I'm fine. Sit. I just need you to be here for me." I said. Already tears were welling up.

"Talk to me, Lady. What's wrong?" He placed an arm around my shoulder and gave me a squeeze. "What's on your mind?"

I laid my head on his shoulder. "KoKo and I got into it. I hate when we argue. Kind of feel guilty about it." I said, thumbing my gold charmed necklace.

"What happened?" He asked.

"She called me a Pick-Me." I answered, ready to explain what a Pick-Me was.

Isaac chuckled.

I lifted my head to look at him. "What?"

"Nothing. Why do you feel guilty?" He asked.

"I don't know." I shrugged. "I hate confrontations."

"You know what your problem is? You're too much of a people-pleaser. Fuck what everyone else thinks. Fuck how they feel. You need to do what's best for Ivonne."

"I'm not a people-pleaser." I said, offended.

"Okay." Isaac responded, refusing to debate with me.

I sniffled. "Then she tried to say that Adrian tried to hit on her. First of all, Adrian doesn't even like dark-skinned women."

"Did you tell her that?"

I shook my head. "No, I didn't wanna hurt her feelings. You know how sensitive some of our people are about complexion."

Again, he chuckled. "KoKo is the unofficial spokeswoman for all dark chocolate sistas out here just by breaking barriers in the urban world. From what I know of her from the media and in real life, that shit wouldn't have bothered her. I can bet she's very secure in herself. She's a trendsetter with millions of men and women gawking over her. She'll always be *Koreen the Dream* to me, though." Isaac admitted with a goofy look in his eyes.

I jabbed his rib with my elbow.

"Ow!"

"Will you focus? I drove all this way for a shoulder to cry on. I can't talk to Adrian about this. He'll ask me to drop my friendship with KoKo."

KOKO

"I knew it!" Isaac exclaimed. "He *is* trying to isolate you. Can't you see that?"

"I have no idea what you're talking about, Isaac."

"Yes, you do. You deserve better. You shouldn't have to end your friendships or change who you are just to keep someone. You understand where I'm coming from?"

"I understand what you're trying to say, but that's not me. I do what I want and I'm happy with Adrian."

"No arguments? Nothing?"

I gave a him a prideful smile. "None. I love that man." I said earnestly.

Isaac groaned.

I giggled. "What was that for?" I asked, interlocking my arm with his.

"I'm certain that the reason why there aren't any disagreements is because you go along with everything he says. Look, you need a man who will put in the effort to be with you. He should be the one chasing *you*, not the other way around."

"Now wait a minute. I don't have to chase. I've already got him."

"You say that so proudly." He shook his head. "You're doing unnecessary shit to try to keep him. You've even coverted to Catholicism for this dude! I can't even get you to give veganism a try. I can bet my entire life savings that so far, you've been the one proving yourself to him."

I didn't answer.

He continued. "The man for you will love you just as you are, Ivonne. I know income and occupation is important to you, Von, but when that real man comes along, he will see past your wealth, occupation, and your beauty. Trust me. You're a beautiful person. You just need to discover that within you."

I couldn't say anything. Some of what he had just said rang true. However, I was still sure that Adrian and I were in this for the long haul. He wasn't like the others before him.

"In other news, I like your hair." Isaac complimented, running his fingers through the long-layered mane that I had traded in my professional shoulder-length bob for.

"Thank you. I decided to let my hair grow out." Plus, Adrian had mentioned that he had always dated women with naturally long hair, but I wasn't about to tell Isaac that.

He moved his face near my neck and inhaled. "Smell good, too. What is that? Guilty by Gucci?"

"Good guess."

"Not really." He replied, carefully holding my hair away from my neck. He brought his face in closer to my jaw and inhaled. "I just know what you like." He added. The breath from his words tickled my neck pleasantly.

The feel of Isaac's full soft lips lightly planting a kiss on my bare neck surprised me. "I pay attention." He stated in a low voice, right before planting a series of soft kisses that travelled from my collarbone to my earlobe.

I was about to protest, when he continued in a whisper. "You've always been my dream woman."

KOKO

He confessed in between kisses that had now found their way to my chin.

I closed my eyes as I leaned my head back.

"I'll always be in love with you, Ivonka. You'll always be mine in my heart." He whispered, right before our lips touched and greeted one another.

CHAPTER TWENTY
KoKo

Today would mark the beginning of my redemption for my previous reality show, *Koreen Unfiltered*. The camera crew were scheduled to arrive in just a couple of hours to begin production for my wedding special, *A Dream's Wedding*. I wasn't too crazy about the name. In fact, I felt like the network were hurting my brand by incorporating the word Dream in the name, knowing that I had buried "Koreen the Dream" years ago. Ivonka tried her best to get the network to settle on an alternative name. We had proposed *KoKo Gets Married* or even *KoKo: A Dream's Wedding*, but the powers-that-be wouldn't budge. I decided to let the issue go when my agent, Irene, convinced me that since *Koreen the Dream* was associated with prior scandals, everyone would be tuning in to see *A Dream's Wedding*, expecting to find drama. She explained that I could use the platform to show how much I had grown. I could only hope that she was right.

I was so excited about the first day of filming, that I was up bright and early. I felt like a kid on Christmas morning.

"Mmmm, it's five in the morning, babe. What are you doing?" Pierre asked, using one eye to squint at the digital clock on our nightstand.

KOKO

I giggled mischievously. I pulled out his sleeping dick from out the peephole of his Calvin Kline boxers. "What does it feel like I'm doing?"

With my face between his thighs, I teased the head of his dick with my flicking tongue. I then glided my mouth up and down the sides of my fiancé's shaft, while softly caressing and cupping his balls with my hand. My lips produced a popping sounding while I sucked the head of his dick. When his dick finally started to stiffen, that was encouragement enough for my mouth to devour his firm cock whole.

"Mmmm." He moaned. I was surprised but pleased to feel the pressure of his hand on top of my pink bonnet. Knowing that I was turning him on, was further turning me on.

"*Mmmm. Shit!*" He moaned again when I spat on his balls and began devouring them as well. I was further surprised when he didn't try to stop me as he often did in the past.

With my right hand stroking his humongous dick up and down, I began humming while I continued sucking on his balls. It was something new I had learned from Ganja. The vibration of the humming always drove him crazy and with the way Pierre was moaning and touching me, I could tell it was turning him on, too.

I lifted me face away from his boxers. "Pull your leg up." I instructed.

"What? Why you stop?" He asked groggily.

"Put your feet flat on the bed, like this." I bent his right leg, then pushed his foot flat on the bed.

Pierre chuckled. "Why do I feel like I'm about to have a baby?"

The mention of the word 'baby' was a brief reminder that Pierre still didn't have a clue that I was 7 weeks pregnant. I quickly pushed the thought out my mind and focused on enjoying my husband-to-be.

It was my turn to moan while I deep-throated his monster-sized dick. My pussy had long begun to moisten and felt like it was now dripping wet with secretion. I spat on his dick and slowly bobbed my head up and down, delighted by the taste of precum in my mouth. Locking my eyes with his, my tongue travelled down to his scrotum again.

He released another moan.

Pleased with how this was going, I continued to jack him off, allowing my tongue to travel further south.

"Wait, hey what are you doing?" Pierre's body grew rigid as my tongue made its way towards his anus.

"Yo, stop that!" He sat up, pushing his tall frame against the head board and away from me, both legs sprawled on top of our floral-printed sheets, as they had been before.

He seemed angry. "Why'd you do that?" He asked.

I smirked. "What? You didn't like it?"

"I'm not gay." He argued.

I laughed. "You don't have to be gay to like it, babe. You should be comfortable with your sexuality." I thought of Biggz, who had thoroughly enjoyed it when I had done the same to him during our last sexual encounter a week ago.

Pierre was not amused. "I'm serious, KoKo. That shit's not cool."

I laughed even harder and Pierre began stuffing his now limp dick back into his boxers.

"Wait, I ain't done yet." I protested, then slapped his hands away from his crotch.

"Well, that stunt you pulled put him to sleep." Pierre stated.

"Don't worry, I can wake him up." I assured, putting his soft dick back in my mouth.

Within a few minutes of showing off my superb fellatio, Pierre was ready to erupt.

"Cum on my face baby, pleeaaaase." I begged. I was on my stomach laying between his thighs again, watching him jack his dick while I cupped his balls. Pierre's face scrunched up in a grimace as he quickened his pace.

"Cum for me, daddy. Cum on my face." I purred.

Pierre released a low growl as semen began to spurt out the eye of his dick, resembling an angry volcano. I pulled my face closer to his dick, attempting to catch his cum, but he pushed me away. I watched in disappointment as he cupped his hand over the head of his dick to block any more of his semen from flying out.

"You know it creeps me out when you call me daddy." He reminded me between breaths of air.

Feeling once again annoyed and defeated, I crawled off the bed in silence and headed for the shower. I had really tried to put in effort this morning to satisfy my sexual appetite with my fiancé by exerting all my focus on pleasing him and it hadn't worked.

By the time I came out the shower with my robe on, Jada was sitting on top of our bed Indian-style in her yellow pajamas. They were both laughing at a cartoon show on the television set.

"There's coffee downstairs." Pierre informed, taking a sip from his *World's Greatest Dad* coffee mug.

"Morning, Jada. Where's mommy's hug?" I asked J'adore, as I stood at the foot of the king-sized bed with my arms spread.

"*Goo mawning, mommy!*" My 3-year-old jumped up from the bed to hug me, causing Pierre to almost spill his coffee.

I gave her a tight embrace, then fingered the two disheveled ponytails on her head.

I shot Pierre a stern look. "What happened to Toya? Wasn't she supposed to do Jada's hair yesterday?"

Pierre raised both brows and shrugged.

"I can't have my daughter on T.V. looking a hot mess." I said with an attitude.

J'adore frowned. "I'm not a hot mess."

Pierre laughed.

"Look, I got some shit to handle but you need to call Toya and tell her to bring her ass over here to do Jada's hair before the production crew gets here."

"We still have plenty of time." Pierre reassured nonchalantly. "They won't be here until noon. It's only 7. It shouldn't take that long to do her hair. Isn't that right bean-head?" He teased our daughter.

"*You're a bean head!*" J'adore exclaimed as she leaped in her father's arm.

I sighed. "At least we got yours out the way." I said, glancing at the intricately twisted and designed coif that our hairstylist, Toya, had styled Pierre's locs.

"Well, I'll be back. I have some last-minute errands to run before they get here. Make sure you clean out the coffeepot and turn on the dishwasher. J'adore make sure you keep your room clean. Don't take any toys out until tomorrow."

J'adore frowned. "What about Elmo?"

"No Elmo." I reiterated. "I'll call Toya and let her know Jada needs her hair done ASAP."

After hanging up with Toya, I quickly slipped into my favorite sheer floral Dolce & Gabbana sundress. I pulled off my bonnet and added a few crinkles to my bone-straight bright pink tresses that fell right below my butt.

I planted kisses on my fiancé's and daughter's forehead before rushing out the door. As soon as I was safely inside my Royce, I pulled out my phone and sent a text.

U HOME? 7:34am
YEAH WHATS UP SEXY 7:34am
IM ON MY WAY 7:35am

***

"*Wha gwan, baby girl?*" Ganja greeted me in his Jamaican accent about a half an hour later at his hotel suite. He was as naked as the day he was born with a fat blunt hanging out the side of his mouth.

"I need some dick." I said frankly, after giving him a smooch on the lips. "Oh, and Moet's on the way. She said it would be no longer than ten minutes."

"I gotchu baby girl. Don't worry. Come in, come in." He extended the door open.

"Look like the party already started without us." I said, eyeing two beautiful dark Caribbean women in the living room area. One sported long braids and the other wore her hair in a short Halle Berry cut. Both were nude and smoking pot on the sofa.

Ganja walked past me and sat between the women. "I'm afraid you were late to the party, my dear, but no fret. We were just about to have an encore."

The two women giggled.

KOKO

CHAPTER TWENTY-ONE
Desi

I wasn't quite sure which happened first: If I had pulled both triggers or was knocked to the ground with my husband's weight on top of me.

"Go! Go! Go!", was all I had heard my husband shouting in Spanish to his mistress, followed by the sound of a vehicle screeching away with a flat tire.

"*Estas loco?* You're lucky she didn't call the police!" Lucas was shouting at the top of his lungs once we were both back inside our home.

"*I'm* lucky?" I asked incredulously.

"You're lucky the neighbors didn't call. That's if they didn't call. The fuckin police could be pulling up any second now."

"Nah, she's lucky I didn't kill her ass! She got some nerve coming here trying to pin a baby on you!" I pointed out, watching him unbutton his long-sleeved shirt.

"Did you take your medication today?" He asked.

I walked up to him, pointing my index finger in his face. "I don't need no fuckin' antidepressants! I need you to stop fucking these nasty bitches!" I shouted in Spanish.

Lucas held my shoulders and stared me in the eyes. "Desi, for once in your life, please believe me when I say I never touched that slut. I don't even like Venezuelans, you know that."

Before I could express my adamant doubt, the short melodic tune of our doorbell sang. Lucas immediately released me and trotted to our bedroom window and peered below.

"Is it the cops?" I asked anxiously. Images of my children and weeping mother flashed before my eyes. His body released a deep breath. "It's your friend."

I rushed over to the window besides Lucas. Relief swept over me upon seeing a blue Jetta instead of a Miami Beach Police cruiser. I retrieved my wallet and iPhone from the nightstand and headed downstairs.

"Oh, hey! I'm sorry, were you heading out?" Jennifer Gray, a mother of one of the boys on my eldest son's soccer team, asked. Her bright blue eyes travelled up and down my long red evening gown. She looked every bit of a soccer mom with blonde shoulder-length tousled hair, a stained white tee, and frumpy "mom" jeans.

I gave her a broad smile. "We just got in. Come in." I said, holding the door open.

"You look gorgeous." She praised. We exchanged air-kisses on both cheeks.

"Thank you, Jen."

"I tried calling and texting you first. Never got a response but I knew how much you needed these so I thought why not stop by on my way to the cleaners?" She explained as she walked past me and stood in my living room. She never stayed long enough to sit when she came by.

"Oh, no, you're fine. We were out celebrating my husband's birthday. Had so much going on, didn't hear my phone. Especially with the baby and all. I'm so happy you stopped by. I totally forgot." I said.

"Here you go. *40* milligrams. Ninety-day supply." She handed over an orange vial in exchange for the eighteen folded up Benjamins I had retrieved from my wallet. I waited as she counted the money.

"I really do appreciate you stopping by, Jen." I said, burying the vial in my cleavage.

"It's nothing. Be sure to wish Mr. Loren a happy birthday for me." She said before leaving.

"Will do."

I dumped the 90 tablets of Hydrocodone in a Zoloft prescription bottle. After my first attempt at suicide, I was prescribed Zoloft by a psychiatrist. Lucas was under the impression that I had been getting refills of Zoloft every ninety days.

My phone buzzed notifying me of a new text. I rolled my eyes at the sight of the message from KoKo:

DESI CALL ME. I NEED U.

No sooner did I delete the text did another message come through from KoKo:

IM PREG. NOT SURE ITS HUBBYS. CALL ME DESI. PLEASE.

I felt a twinge of guilt when I ignored the second text, but quickly dismissed it. Koreen put herself in this predicament and she needed to face the consequences. As a matter of fact, she had some nerve hating Lucas. They were both two lying cheating whores in a relationship with people too good for them. Again, the thought of setting KoKo's ass up to expose to Pierre the type of woman he was about to marry crossed my mind. If I had his number

I probably would've sent him a screenshot. I felt compassion for him. I didn't want him wasting away his life and marriage on a lie like I had done.

"Des, the boys just called from your mother's. They wanna come home." I heard Lucas call out from upstairs.

I didn't answer. I opened the orange vial and placed two tablets on my tongue. I quickly swallowed, then headed upstairs to change into comfortable jeans, a t-shirt, and Air Jordans.

"Where you going?" Lucas asked when I grabbed the keys to the SUV. He was laying on our California king sized bed with just his boxers on, flicking through the channels with the remote control.

"Didn't you say the boys were ready to come home?" I asked with an attitude. "If I don't go get them who else gonna pick them up?"

Lucas grunted in annoyance before answering. "You know your mother hates me. I'm not stepping foot in her run-down apartment."

"I don't see why we can't get a nanny. KoKo and Pierre have one and they only got J'adore." I complained.

"She works. You don't do shit around here all day." He tried rebutting, his eyes glued to the T.V. I placed a hand on my hip as I snarled at the old son-of-a-bitch. "Oh, for real? You don't think I do shit all day?"

He finally broke his gaze from the television screen to look at me. "You sit around on your ass all day while the kids are in school. The house is always a mess and you barely have food ready when I get home. What the fuck do you do all day, hunh? Other than gossip with those sluts on the phone. A married woman shouldn't only have single ladies as friends."

"I'll find a job then and go back to school." I said, already knowing what his response would be.

He sat up. "School for *what*?" He started in Spanish. "Once I'm dead, you and the kids will be set for life. You don't need no fuckin school and what job will hire you with no work experience? The only work you've ever done was shake your ass in music videos. What are you gonna do, become a stripper? Over my dead body, not my wife!"

"Well, it's either we get a nanny or…"
Lucas laughed, then shook his head pitifully at me.

"Or what? What? You're gonna leave? Who's gonna want you? Twenty-four with 6 kids and no education. All the beautiful women in this world, who would choose you with all that baggage? Where you gonna house six kids? Idiot. Get real. Just know, you ever decide to leave or divorce, your ass is not getting a dime from me!"

"Fuck you, you old piece of shit!" I spat. I grabbed my purse then stormed out of our bedroom before he could say anything else.

His words stung and my eyes welled up with tears as I slammed the front door in frustration. I felt trapped in this marriage. I also felt like I had been tricked into this miserable life. I just wanted Lucas to stop fucking other women and I wanted to be happy.

I pulled out of our long narrow driveway and drove up to the stop sign down the street from our small mansion. Hearing sirens in the distance, I checked my rear-view mirror. My heart stopped as I watched three Miami Beach police cruisers about a half a yard behind me speeding towards me with flashing red and blue lights. Paralyzed with fear, I observed as all three cruisers slowed down, then make a right turn towards my drive way.

Somehow I managed to floor the gas pedal, nearly hitting an elderly man on a bicycle. I grabbed my phone from my purse and dialed Ivonne's number with trembling fingers as soon as I stopped at a red light. I figured I needed a lawyer and a friend right about now.

Someone answered the phone but it wasn't Ivonka. "Hello?" The gruff voice belonged to a man and did not sound friendly. In fact, he sounded annoyed.

I glanced at my phone to make sure I had dialed the right number. I had. "Is this Ivonka's number?"

"She's in the shower right now. How may we help you?" He asked. I was assuming the guy on the line was Ivonne's best friend from back home, Isaac.

"Can you please tell her to call Desiree? It's important. I may be in jail soon and need her help. Please have her call me ASAP."

"Sorry sweetheart but those days of using my woman for money are over. Don't call this phone again." He said. I was about to curse his ass out and inform him that my husband made more than enough money and that I needed her to get me a defense attorney, but the asshole had already hung up.

KOKO

"Shit!" I balled my right hand into a fist and slammed it against the dashboard.

My phone rang just as I decided to pull into the parking lot of a grocery store. Praying it was Ivonne, I answered without glancing at the caller I.D.

"Desiree, *dónde estás?* The police are here looking for you." I heard my mom's worried voice ask.

"It's okay, mami. I don't need the boys worrying either." I stated.

"What did you do to that woman, Desi? Why are they looking for you?" She asked.

"I didn't do anything to her." I lied. "Can you keep the kids tonight please, while I take care of this?"

She ignored my question as she began to rant, "That Lucas! I bet your father is rolling over in his grave! He knew that man was trouble from the moment we laid eyes on him. What would a man his age need with an 18-year-old girl? No morals!"

"Mami, I have to go." I said, as tears started to well up in my eyes again.

I pulled in a parking space toward the back of the parking lot and sniffled as my mother continued,

"Your sister, Delores, has a good respectable husband...*what?*" I could hear voices in the background. "Desi, baby, I'm going to pass the police the phone now. They want to speak to you, okay?"

I immediately ended the call, then powered off my phone, just in case they tried some sneaky shit like trace my location with my cell phone.

"I'm tired of this shit!" With tears blurring my vision, I threw my iPhone somewhere on the passenger-side floor.

Sick and tired of feeling sick and tired, I wailed in anguish at my current predicament. This shit wasn't fair! Why was this happening to *me*? Why did it seem like the bad guys always won? My ass was about to be locked up while the people who hurt others, like Lucas and KoKo, got to live a life without suffering. What the fuck had I ever done to deserve a life such as this? I had never wronged anyone or cheated on anyone in my life. Lucas had been the only man I had ever been with. Why did God hate me?

"*Whyyyy??!*" I cried as I banged my head on the steering wheel.

I had nothing to look forward to in my life except more pregnancies. I thought of how Lucas and I had made love this morning without protection. I hadn't even been in the mood to fuck him but he mentioned that it was his birthday and then made some slick comment under his breath about getting pleased elsewhere. He always hid my birth control and he never wore condoms. KoKo had suggested long ago that I get my tubes tied after the birth of Luke, my fourth child, and I should've listened. Why bring more kids in the world to suffer? My head was hurting from crying as I thought about how my children had fucked-up parents. I envied my sister, Delores, with her picture-perfect family, her doctoral degree and her successful career. Didn't I deserve happiness too? She had done everything right in my parents' eyes. I never even had the chance to prove myself to my father before his untimely death three years ago. I had made nothing of my life. I felt like nothing. I *was* nothing. What was the point in living? I didn't want to live.

Drowning in a feeling of hopelessness and defeat, I rummaged through my Michael Kors bag until I found both the orange vial and light blue rosary I was looking for.

With the vial safely cupped in my right hand and the rosary draped between the fingers of my left hand, I looked out the front window towards the night sky.

"*Por favor perdoname*. Please forgive me, Father." I pleaded tearfully. "I just don't know what else to do." I added, before opening the vial and emptying its content in the palm of my hand.

CHAPTER TWENTY-TWO
Ivonne

"Who was that, babe?" I asked Adrian as I tied the sash of my terry cloth robe.

"Who?' I thought I heard him ask me as he stood in front of the chifforobe mirror adjusting his tie. I could barely hear him over the blaring television.

I turned down the volume then headed towards my cell phone lying on the bed. "I thought I heard you on the phone. I know I heard my phone ringing."

"No one. Just a bill collector." He answered coolly.

I laughed. "A bill collector? For *me*?" I almost reminded him that everything I owned was paid for but decided against it.

Ever since I had confronted him about a nude picture message from a "Cassandra" I had found on his phone a week ago, Adrian had become more and more paranoid. You would've thought that it had been my phone filled with sexually explicit texts and photos. He claimed he had allowed his friend, Keon, to use his phone and that the messages from this Cassandra person were for Keon.

"They had the wrong number. I took care of it." He said sternly. He began brushing the salt and peppered waves on his head. "You sure you'll be ready in twenty minutes? You know how you women take forever to get dressed."

I walked to where he stood in front of the mirror and hugged him from behind. Not only did my man look good, but he smelled good as well. "I'm sure."

"Come on now, Ivonka. Quit foolin' around and get dressed. How does it look for us to arrive after them folks?" He snapped.

"Alright, alright." I released my man from my grasp and made my way towards my armoire. I knew he was just nervous. I didn't bother explaining to him that entertainers were known to arrive fashionably late, especially musicians.

My prospective client tonight was Armani Rayne, the hottest up-and-coming R&B sensation to come out of Atlanta. With dance moves as sensual as Ciara, lyrics as racy as Nicki Minaj, and a beauty like Rihanna, Armani was considered a triple threat; a Beyoncé in the making. She had hired Pierre to keep her in shape and was looking to replace her current attorney. Pierre had been considerate enough to refer the songstress my way for legal representation.

Other than KoKo, it would be the first time that Adrian would be rubbing elbows with a celebrity and I thought it was cute how excited he had been when I told him Armani and her manager had wanted to have dinner with us. As a matter of fact, my baby was the one who had set up the reservations at Trendy Indies. He had suggested we invite them over for dinner but I quickly rejected that idea. Adrian still had no idea that I could barely boil a pot of water. I had fired my cook Stefan, with pay, a couple of weeks after Adrian had moved in. Thanks to YouTube, I learned to cook a few dishes but for the most part, I had been buying dinner before Adrian arrived from work and passing it as homemade dinners. I had stashed a notebook full of recipes from YouTube that seemed easy to put together. I wanted to prove to my man that I was wife-material and I wanted to do it quickly. My 38th birthday was just a couple of months away and I was hoping to be engaged by next year. My plan was to be engaged by the end of the year and pregnant by my 39th birthday.

"We look great together, don't we?" Adrian asked as he wrapped his arms around my waist from behind me and stared at our reflection in the mirror.

I blushed and nodded. With my man outfitted in a navy Versace suit and myself in a navy Dolce & Gabbana fitted dress, I thought we complimented each other perfectly.

I could feel his prickly hairs from his salt-and-peppered goatee when he kissed me on the neck. "You're so beautiful."

"Thank you, baby." I blushed. Adrian had a way of making me feel beautiful and worthy of affection.

All of the disappointments from my past relationships had been worth it. He was perfect in my eyes and very well worth the wait. The fact that a man as sweet and handsome as Adrian adored *me*, helped me to feel validated. He helped me to feel like there was nothing wrong with me. He always reminded me that I wasn't the reason why I had never been married or had children. He said the guys from my past didn't recognize a jewel when they seen one. Adrian helped me in loving myself and I loved him for it. I did everything in my power to keep him happy. I wasn't about to lose my man. I loved him and didn't know what would happen to me if he ever left me. Deep down, I felt like I would never find another man as handsome and loving as Adrian. He was definitely 'the one'.

Just as I expected, Armani Rayne arrived a little after a half an hour. I was a little surprised to see her accompanied not by her manager or bodyguard, but by Pierre.

Television and magazine spreads did no justice for Armani's beauty. The songstress was even more breathtaking in person. Her hazel contacts complimented her warm honey-toned complexion perfectly, reminding me of a shiny new penny. Her workouts with Pierre were doing her body right. I thought I even caught Adrian admiring the young woman's curves and toned stature in a tight yellow - leather mini dress. With a woman as stunning as Armani, I couldn't help wondering how KoKo felt about Pierre working alone with her so often. I quickly dismissed that thought. KoKo was one of the most self-confident women I had ever run across. Besides, she had once bragged that Pierre was only into dark toned women anyway.

I greeted both Armani and Pierre with a firm handshake. "Did you guys find the place okay?" I asked Armani.

Her eyes twinkled as she exposed a set of perfectly white teeth. "Yes, we were able to find this place with no issue thanks to Pierre. I almost cancelled because Freddy, my manager, had to be rushed to the emergency room and couldn't make it tonight. Freddy insisted that I go with Pierre instead." She replied, flashing Pierre a smile and wink.

"Oh, is he okay?" I asked, concerned.

"He's okay. We think it's food poisoning. I warned him about buying shrimp on the side of the road."

Sitting beside me, Adrian cleared his throat.

"Oh, where are my manners?" I said. "This is my boyfriend Adrian Michaels. Adrian, this is Armani Rayne and Pierre Woods. You remember KoKo, don't you babe? Pierre and KoKo are engaged." I said as they greeted each other.

Dinner with Armani and Pierre went as planned without a hitch. Adrian and I were pleased when she agreed to hire me as her attorney.

"I don't know about you, but I am exhausted babe." I released a yawn.

"I hear you, so am I." Adrian said. "I'm so proud of you, Ivonka." He said as he helped me unzip my dress.

"I didn't do anything. That was all Pierre. I'm gonna have to send him a thank you card or something in the morning."

Adrian grunted then clicked the television on. I didn't bother asking him what that was about. I had a feeling he didn't care too much about Pierre or KoKo. Adrian had barely spoken to him when Pierre tried to make conversation with him.

After washing my make-up off in the bathroom, I entered the bedroom and Adrian jumped as if I had scared him. I was about to ask him what was up

KOKO

when I heard Mindy Mathers voice from the television.

"What is that wench gossiping about now?" I asked, sitting beside Adrian. "Turn the volume up, babe." I said to Adrian.

"How many of you remember KoKo's previous reality show, Koreen Unfiltered?" Mindy asked and the camera panned to a sea of faces in the audience. A chorus of yes and no's rang out from the audience.

Mindy continued. *"Well it looks like that circus is back in town."*

I shook my head as the audience laughed and applauded the popular Asian host with the black NBA star husband, as she took a sip of tea from her baby blue teacup. As usual, Mindy's oversized bosoms were barely covered in a loud form-fitting bright green dress. Her super-straight long blonde extensions were draped over one shoulder as she began to divulge 'the tea' to the audience.

"If the new reality show is anything like Koreen Unfiltered, I'll definitely be tuning in. Y'all know Mindy loves the filth, honey, and that KoKo is definitely messy."

A few claps and laughs could be heard from the audience.

"Honeeeey the show hasn't even aired yet and the mess has already begun, y'all." Mindy said animatedly. *"According to the Daily Tea, a reliable source has confirmed that the video vixen is pregnant!"*

My heart sped as a chorus of surprised 'oooohs' sang out from the audience.

"I'll change the channel." Adrian stated, aiming the remote towards the screen.

I grabbed his arm. "Hold on a minute, babe."

"And the baby's father isn't even the man she's marrying on the show, y'all!" Mindy exclaimed.

Mindy waited for the cries of outrage and judgement to die down from the audience before continuing, *"I don't know, y'all. This story has 'publicity stunt' written all over it. Can we put up the picture of Ms. Thang and her hubby-to-be?"*

A photo of KoKo and Pierre seated at Le Duce appeared on a large screen behind the host.

"Isn't he a snack? How did she land a fox like that? For those of you who don't know, his name is Pierre Woods and he's a well-known personal trainer in the entertainment industry. Look at that body, y'all."

Mindy seemed to be salivating as a photo of Pierre at the beach in swimwear appeared next on the screen behind her. Pierre appeared to be holding a beach bag under his arm. KoKo was right behind him in a white two-piece holding on to little J'adore's hand.

"I love a man with locs. That's why I married one!" She held up her hand, showing off the rock on her ring finger, then took another sip of tea. *"Well anyway, back to the queen of messy herself, Koreen the Dream. Mr. Pierre Woods, honey, if you're watching this please understand that you can't turn a ho into a housewife."*

The audience erupted in astonished laughter. Adrian chuckled.

Mindy laughed. *"Oh, stop it, y'all. That was no shade. I don't need her fans harassing me, either. Every time someone says something about 'Miss.Thang', her fans get in their feelings. Look, I admit Koreen's a very* beautiful girl but let's face it: she can change her name to KoKo, but she will always be messy ass Koreen the Dream to those of us in the industry who really know her. Don't believe me? Ask Stormy Knight or Keyshia Valentine why they stopped affiliating with Ms. KoKo. They'll tell you."

The audience snickered. I shook my head in disgust. I knew for a fact that KoKo and the two ladies were still very good friends.

"Well anyway according to a reliable source, the vixen is allegedly pregnant and the father could be any-damn-body, including her homosexual ex-husband, Bernard 'Lyrical Bernz' Ingram! We'll see

if Ms. Koreen the Dream and Mr. Woods make it to the altar." The audience gasped again as Mindy nodded her head with a grin.

My cell phone rang and I grabbed it before Adrian could.

Still in a state of shock, I quickly answered without checking my caller I.D. "Hello?"

"Are you that miserable, bitch?" A woman's voice shouted from the other end of the phone.

"KoKo?" I asked, looking down at my phone. I quickly checked the caller ID and confirmed that it was indeed KoKo.

"If I lose this endorsement with Melanin Cosmetics because of this shit, I'm kickin in yo door, bitch!"

"Now wait a minute, Koreen. I did not leak that story. What reason would I have? I have more money than I know what to do with-"

"You a miserable jealous BITCH!" She shouted.

"Jealous?" I was stunned.

"You jealous of my man, my confidence, my youth, my pregnancies, and my engagement! You a sorry ass miserable old bitch!"

I was getting angry. She wasn't even trying to hear me. "Old? Me jealous of *you*? You're barely a parent, KoKo. J'adore sees Teresa more than she sees you." I said, referring to the nanny she and Pierre had hired when J'adore was just a few weeks old. "You're too busy flying around the country whoring around to even spend time with Pierre, let alone J'adore!"

KoKo interjected. "It's called *living*, bitch. You ain't here with me and mine 24 hours a day. I spend time with my family, you miserable Pick-Me! You should try it sometimes instead of always moping around about how you can't find a husband and spreading your legs to losers. You so caught up in proving your worth to these lame ass niggas that you lettin' life pass you by! Always end up lookin' pitiful as fuck!"

"I can't find a man? What in the world are you talkin about? I have a man-" I started to say.

She interrupted again. "That old ass nothin nigga that you kicked your best friend out for? That nigga tried to feel me up, bitch!"

"He tried to feel you up?" I repeated in disbelief

Adrian grabbed the phone. "Look whore," Adrian said, "Why don't you go find out who your baby's father is instead of harassing us?" I could hear KoKo shouting from the other end.

Adrian face turned a crimson color as he bellowed, "You walk around like you're the big bad wolf but you aint gonna do shit, bitch! *No, fuck you!*

I'm from the streets of Chicago! Cabrini Green projects, ho! I ain't one of these Florida boys around here, bitch!"

I couldn't believe what was happening. I rubbed my throbbing head before grabbing my cell phone back from Adrian.

"Look, Koreen, it *wasn't* me." I said earnestly just as my other line beeped.

I glanced quickly glanced at my caller ID as KoKo continued with her expletives. I did a double take when Desiree's name appeared across my screen.

"KoKo, I'm gonna have to call you back. Desi's beeping in." I said, hoping that would change her attitude a bit.

"I bet she is. She don't fuck with me no more. You two were supposed to be my maid of honors. Fuck you and that druggie! I can't trust none of you bitches!"

I gasped. "Wow, KoKo. I'm gonna hang up and let you cool down before we both end up saying some things we'll regret."

"Naw, fuck that!" KoKo bellowed indignantly.

"Y'all miserable bitches set me up! Fuck y'all. I mean everything I say. As a matter of fact, both of y'all miserable bitches could die tonight, I wouldn't give a FUCK!"

Shaking my head, I clicked over to my other line.

"Desi?" I greeted anxiously. "Where in the world have you been, girl?!" I had truly missed my friend.

On the end I could hear weeping.

"Hello?" I said again.

"Ivonne?" I heard a woman's voice say. I could barely hear the woman between her sobs and sound of blaring sirens in the background.

It wasn't Desiree's voice.

"Who is this? Where's Desiree?"

"Ivonne, it's Gloria, Desi's mother."

I could feel myself about to have an anxiety attack. "Oh my God. Did something happen to Desiree?"

I could see Adrian staring at me. "What's going on?" He mouthed.

I ignored him as Gloria explained. "I don't know. I'm outside of Mount Sinai Hospital. They think she overdosed."

"What?"

"Please, Ivonka, I need you to come get the children. They don't need to be here. That sorry Lucas isn't answering his phone. Probably out with another woman. Piece of trash! He drove her to this!' She began sobbing again.

"Gloria, I'll be there in about 15 minutes." I reassured.

Adrian was still looking at me when I ended the call. "What was that all about?"

"Desiree's in the hospital. I gotta go pick up the kids." I explained while slipping on a pair of jeans and a t-shirt.

"Word? What happened?" He asked.

"I don't know. Where are my keys? What are you doing?" I asked, as I watched him put on his sneakers.

"I'm coming with you."

I sighed. "There might not be enough space in the car for all of us." I pointed out.

"How many of them are there?" He asked.

"Six."

He grunted, then mumbled something about kids making a mess in the mansion. I ignored it and gave him a kiss on the forehead.

"I'll be back within the hour."

CHAPTER TWENTY-THREE
KoKo

I was so on edge, that I didn't give a fuck about the slew of paparazzi waiting outside Mount Sinai Hospital when I arrived. Somehow, those motherfuckers had been able to spot me even with my shades and my long hair tucked underneath a fitted Miami Heat cap. Hospital security pushed the crowd back as I was escorted inside the hospital.

"I'm here to see Desiree Loren." I informed the white woman at the front desk.

She handed me a visitor's pass to stick on to my t-shirt, then asked if I wanted one of the security guards to escort me to Desi's room. I nodded graciously at the woman. She summoned over a tall white buff guy and instructed him to accompany me to the psych ward

I crinkled my forehead in confusion. *Psych ward?* Too many thoughts and emotions were racing through me. I thought that maybe I had heard wrong. With Ivonka backstabbing me, Pierre not coming home and ignoring my calls, and Desi in the hospital, my mind was all over the place. I felt as if I could have a mental breakdown of my own at any minute.

"They're gonna have to turn off those cameras, ma'am." The woman informed.

I had completely forgotten that the camera crew were still filming. I followed the beefy security guard as the crew stayed behind to take a much- needed break. They had been filming for the past 9 hours. As a matter of fact, I had gotten so used to being filmed, that half the time I forgot they were there and I had to be very careful with that. Biggz had been blowing up my phone non-stop since the pregnancy story had leaked. I couldn't answer for fear of being exposed by the show. I knew from past experience that the producers had no mercy when it came to scandal. I had even almost gotten caught speaking to Ganja today. His ass had called to let me know that he had heard on the radio that I was pregnant. The asshole had the nerve to warn me not to even think about pinning the baby on him because he wasn't paying a dime of child support. Meanwhile, the one person I had been waiting to hear from all day wasn't returning my calls or text messages.

 I needed to be able to gauge how Pierre felt about the pregnancy rumors, especially since he hadn't even known I was pregnant to begin with. I knew he had met up with Ivonka for dinner and I desperately wanted to call Ivonka to ask about Pierre's whereabouts, but I vowed to never fuck with that backstabbing bitch again. I couldn't understand how she had the audacity to be so adamant about denying it was her who leaked my pregnancy when several media outlets had audio recordings of private phone conversations between her and I. The urban gossip sites were already chewing me up and tearing me a new one.

 "Over here, Ms. Wilson." The security guard's voice shook me from my thought. We had stopped right in front of room 1229, Desiree's room.

"Thank you." I told him.

"Would you mind if I asked for an autograph?" He blurted out hesitantly.

I raised both my brows in surprise. I didn't think he knew who I was.

"Hey, just because I'm white as snow doesn't mean I don't watch hip hop videos or urban movies." The security guard chuckled. "Besides, my daughter and her mother are black."

"Alright, sure." I smiled politely. "What would you like for me to sign?"

He patted his front pocket for a pen. "I think I lost my pen. How about a picture?"

"Didn't they say all phones needed to be powered off on this floor?" I reminded.

He shrugged. "It's okay."

Although I really didn't feel up to par in a Heat cap, jeans, and no make-up, I still allowed him to snap a picture before entering Desiree's room.

"Desi?" I whispered.

I was surprise to see her look over at me with a smile. I had half-expected to see her unconscious with tubes coming out of her nostrils or something.

"Well if it isn't miss thang. Why are you whispering?" She laughed. Oh, how I had missed her signature infectious laugh. I missed my friend so much.

I rushed up to her and gave her the tightest hug I could muster.

She chuckled. "Oh my god, are you really crying, girl?" She teased as I quickly wiped away tears.

I nodded. I wanted to speak but my throat felt so tight, I knew I would burst into tears if I attempted to talk. I wasn't sure if it was the hormones or the fact that I felt like the loneliest person in the world right now.

"I should probably change this." She said. I looked up at the television to see a picture of me and my ex-husband, Bernie, plastered on the screen.

"Yes, please do." I managed to say.

"Are the rumors true?" She asked.

I nodded.

She raised an eyebrow.

"It was only a one-night stand. We were both drunk. I have no intentions of ever sleeping with him again."

She nodded but I wasn't sure if she believed me.

"What are you doing lying in a hospital, much less the psych ward, Desi? And why have you been giving me the cold shoulder? Did I do something to piss you off or somethin'?" I asked sympathetically.

Desiree sighed. "I don't know. I just feel like my life is in shambles. I'm miserable and I feel trapped. You wouldn't understand. I know I have children to live for but I can't live like this."

"Like what?" I asked, still trying to understand.

Her mother had called me an hour ago to tell me that Desi had been rushed to the hospital. She had hung up before I could ask anything else. So to see my friend in a psych ward was very much disturbing.

"I have my own goals and dreams and I'll never be able to reach them. I hate my life. I was the one stealing your vials."

I nodded. "I already knew that."

Again, she raised an eyebrow. "You did?"

"Is that why you been avoiding me?" I asked, ignoring her question.

She looked away ashamedly.

I held her hand. "Girl, you know you my bitch. We supposed to be best friends. There's nothing that you could ever do change that." I said then regretted it, as I thought about Ivonka's trifling ass. "Did Ivonka already stop by?"

Desiree shook her head. "My mom had called her an hour ago to get the kids. She never showed up. My mom is on her way to drop the kids off to my sister's house. I was just about to ask you about Ivonne. Her phone been going straight to voicemail."

I frowned. "I don't fuck with that backstabbing bitch."

Desi shot me a disapproving look. "Please don't tell me you think she had anything to do with the leak. Ivonne would *never* do that."

I shot her my own disapproving look back. "Don't be so naïve, Desiree. I know you've been missin' in action so you'd never understand. That woman has been doing a lot of fucked up shit that I never thought she'd do ever since she hooked up with that Adrian."

"They still together?"

I nodded. "Yes, that desperate bitch is still with that sketchy ass nigga. She done moved his ass in and all."

"Ohhh." Desi said softly, her mouth still hanging open. "That must've been the guy who answered her phone and hung up on me." Desi began to laugh but I didn't find the shit funny at all.

"You called Ivonne?"

She nodded. "Yeah I called right before I overdosed." She looked away again, then continued. "I thought he was Isaac. Have you met him yet?" She asked.

"Who? Isaac or Adrian?"

"I was talkin' about Isaac but have you met either of em?"

I nodded. "Isaac's cool. His ass hadn't even lasted a full month at her house before she kicked him out to move Mr.- Touchy-Feely in."

Desi covered her mouth with her hand, gasping. "Are you serious?"

I cocked my head to the side. "As a muthafuckin' heart attack. I'm used to her switchin up to kiss up to these niggas but she done took it to a whole other level. I'm so through with that bitch."

"Don't say that. Y'all two will be back to shopping and gossiping on the phone again within a month. Mark my words."

I huffed. "I wouldn't spit on that bitch if I seen her on the side of the road on fire. Fuck her! Can we change the subject?"

Desi laughed "How's my god-daughter and Pierre? Is the wedding still on?"

I took in a deep breath before slowly exhaling. I needed a cigarette. "J'adore is fine. Still a daddy's girl. To tell you the truth, I'm hoping the wedding is still on. Pierre had a business dinner with Ivonne and Armani-"

Desi interrupted. "The singer?"

I nodded. "Yeah. He left around 7pm last night and never came back. He's not returning any of my calls or anything. I've left messages from my phone and Teresa's cell phone. I'm about to call his mama if he don't return my calls."

"Teresa?" She looked confused.

I sniffed. "Our nanny."

"Oh, that's right. Well, you really can't be that surprised about this being uncovered, are you? It was bound to happen, KoKo."

I shrugged. "I don't know. I would have liked for it to not be exposed by someone I thought was my best friend. Did Lucas come by?" I asked, changing the subject.

She shook her head. "My mom told him not to. She hates him more now than ever. She thinks it's his fault that I overdosed."

"Well can you blame her? He ain't shit." I spat.

"And you're better? She asked.

I was taken aback. "What do you mean am I better?"

"You may not realize it or ever admit it but you and Lucas are cut from the same cloth. Both of you continue to hurt the people in your corner. Y'all both sleep around. Both continue to risk your families for people who probably don't give a shit about you."

I was angry but fell silent. We had just made up and I didn't want to rock the boat too soon.

Desi stared at me. "Why do you treat Pierre like that? He loves you. I would kill to have a husband like him."

KOKO

I sighed. "You guys always taking up for Pierre. You wouldn't understand."

"Help me to understand then, because truthfully, that's the reason why I stopped fucking with you. You're selfish as fuck, just like Lucas. When I see you, I see him."

Ouch. That stung. "I'm not being satisfied sexually by Pierre." I confessed, than looked around the room in paranoia. I didn't need any more dirt about me or my family in the media.

"Girl aint nobody else in here but me and you've known me long enough to know I would never sell you out. But look, I have an appointment with a psychiatrist tomorrow. Maybe I can get you a referral?"

I crinkled my forehead. "No offense, but I don't need a damn shrink. I ain't crazy. "I said defensively.

"I'm not crazy either, bitch. What I was saying is I can ask my psychiatrist to recommend a relationship therapist. You two may just need couples therapy, KoKo. At least try it out for the sake of J'adore."

I thought about it. "I would need a therapist that's willing to make house visits. I don't need the attention of the razzi."

She smiled knowingly. "I know that, KoKo."

I squeezed Desi's hand. "Promise me something." I said.

"Depends on what it is." Desi replied laughing.

"Don't you ever just disappear from my life again, you hear me? That hurt. You and Ivonne were like my sisters."

Desiree nodded. "Okay. I promise."

"Can I get a hug?" I asked before bending over to give her a hug anyway.

"Are you crying again?" Desi asked as she pulled away from me.

I laughed. "These damn hormones."

***

The camera crew and half the paparazzi were gone by the time I made it back to the parking lot. The production manager for *A Dream's Wedding* left a message stating filming would resume back at the mansion and that the crew were already at location setting up.

I decided to take a moment to call Biggz back as I sped back home.

"Why the fuck have you been avoiding me?!" Biggz spat out as soon as he'd answered.

"Imma need you to watch that bass in your voice." I said firmly.

"Is it my baby?" he asked.

I furrowed my brow then huffed in annoyance. "I don't understand what you asking me right now. Didn't I tell you from jump that this baby may not be yours?"

"You said it was a fifty-fifty chance.'"

I cut him off. "I never said there was a fifty-fifty chance. *You* said that. I just didn't bother correcting you."

"So it's true?" He asked. Sounding like he was about to cry. "The father could be anybody? You been fucking that gay ass nigga again too, bitch?"

KOKO

"Hold up, who the fuck are you callin' a bitch?" I asked, missing Pierre. Pierre had never called me out of my name not even once. I'd be damn if I let this fat nigga disrespect me.

Instead of responding back, Biggz hung up the phone. I reminded myself to give him a call back later and give him a piece of my mind because at the moment, my main focus was making sure this wedding was still on.

Sure enough, just as the director had informed, the film crew's white van were already parked in my driveway when I pulled up. My stomach felt tight with nerves as I slowly made my way to my front door. I didn't want anyone asking me for Pierre's whereabout, especially my daughter.

I slowed down the pace of my stride then halted once I was about a feet away from the door. I wanted to try just once more to reach Pierre.

This time he answered immediately. "What?" He asked irritably. He sounded like he was in his car with the windows down.

"This is what we're doing now? We're not gonna talk about this? You just disappear and ignore my calls?! Your daughter been asking about you all day!" I lied. She had only asked once but I knew J'adore was his world. I was desperate for him to come home.

"Is this what you called me for? To fuss and shout? I don't think I'm ready to talk about this. *Get off the fuckin road!*" Pierre shouted. I could hear the sounds of multiple horns blowing in his background. I was slightly alarmed. Contrast to his mellow and cool-headed temperament, this was a whole new side of my fiancé that I had never witnessed. I barely ever heard him curse.

I exhaled audibly, then lowered my tone. "Please come home so we can talk about this."

"As a matter of fact, I was just on my way." He revealed.

My shoulders straightened anxiously. "You were? How far are you?"

"I should be there in about an hour. I need to come get a few things. I may come get J'adore, too. Lord knows she can't be with the nanny twenty-four hours." He mumbled bitterly.

Over my dead body, I wanted to say. There was no way I was letting J'adore nor Pierre leave tonight. I was determined to keep my family together. We would get through this!

In the meantime, I played along with Pierre. "Okay, I'll have Teresa pack her an overnight bag." I said, knowing I had no intentions of doing so.

"She'll need more than just an overnight bag. Pack enough for a few of days." He instructed before hanging up.

"Please, let me freshen up, first." I spouted out to the videographer and boom operator as soon as I'd made it inside the mansion. "Where's Melany?" I inquired of the on-set makeup artist that I had made sure to include as part of my contract.

"KoKo, we need you in the confessional booth before Mr. Woods arrives." Todd, the short Caucasian production assistant spouted off rapidly.

"Wait, how did you know Pierre was on his way?" I asked suspiciously. I hoped to God these bitches hadn't recorded any of my calls or leaked any of my phone conversations for that matter.

"We spoke to him about an hour ago." Todd answered.

I scrunched up my forehead. "For what? This is *my* show. If you guys need to speak to Pierre, you let *me* know."

"We were following up with Mr. Woods to see if he was still up for this. We need him in the confessional booth after the confrontation, but we need you in there as soon as possible first; for your feelings on the whole scandal and whatnot."

I snapped my neck back in confusion. "The confrontation? What confrontation?"

Todd held up a hand in defense. "Assuming there will be a confrontation between you and your fiancé when he walks in, Miss. Wilson, I don't know. Think you'll be ready in ten?" He asked impatiently.

"I'll try." I replied, sauntering past him towards my guest bedroom, which had temporarily been converted into my hair and make-up area.

Plopping down on the cushioned leather seat in front of Melany, I grumbled, "Where the fuck is Rachel?"

"She should be on her way back with the dress." Melany answered.

"She need to hurry up. These people already irking my damn nerves." I complained, thinking of the eager nineteen-year old I had hired as my temporary personal assistant.

Melany chuckled. "I hear you. So what we doin' today? Want a more natural look?" She asked as she examined the cosmetics lying on a table besides her. I was tempted to ask her to duplicate her hair and make up on me, but decided her sleek blonde bob complemented her bright yellow skin more than it would my dark chocolate hue. Not that I was envious either. After all, I *was* the unofficial spokeswoman for confident dark-toned women everywhere.

"I need my man to remember why he fell in love with me when he sees me today. I want the 24-inch Brazilian lace-front. Curled. No glue. Hit me with some smoky eyes and extra-long lashes. Oh, and these lips gotta be poppin'. Can we do red lips?" I asked, puckering my soft nude lips in the mirror in front of me.

Melany placed a hand on her hip and smiled."Miss, Thang, it is only eleven in the morning. Let's save the smoky eyes, dramatic lashes, and the red lips for evening wear. You're a model. I know you know better. Last thing you need is for Mindy Mathers to dog you about your make up. Plus, the PA already came over her giving me directions to make sure it's quick."

She had a point. "Just make sure I look sexy."

"Chile, they don't call me the crème de la crème out of Atlanta for nothin'. You gotta trust me." She reassured.

I nodded. "I trust you. I just need a cigarette. Where in the hell is Rachel?"

Melany pointed her chin towards the bedroom door. "There she is."

Rachel's skinny ass rushed in holding a garment bag. She looked winded and disheveled. Her long hair was pulled back in a loose ponytail and her thick oversized glasses were sitting at the tip of her nose.

"That better be the Givenchy." I snapped. Rachel used her index finger to push her glasses back and nodded. "It is." She assured.

She carefully unzipped the garment bag and delicately retrieved a coral lace dress and a pair of my favorite sparkly silver diamond-studded Giuseppe Zanotti stilettos. She then pulled out a pack of Newport lights and handed it to me before I could ask.

"Aren't you pregnant?' Melany asked.

I slammed the pack of cigarettes on top of the cosmetic table in front of me. Melany had just as much spunk and attitude as I did and I didn't feel like going back and forth with her.

"Ms. Wilson, we need you in the living-room right now." Todd instructed hastily, just as Melany had successfully slayed my hair and make-up.

"What about the confessional? Y'all don't want me to do that first?" I asked, confused.

"We have no time. He's here."

"He's here? Already?" I asked, glancing at the time on my iPhone.

"We need you to slip on the dress and answer the door please." Todd said as he rushed past me.

I carefully slipped on the Givenchy dress and heels, then hurried to the livingroom. I was nervous as I thought about how I should greet Pierre or what I would even say but one thing I knew for sure: there was no way he was leaving this mansion with his or J'adore's bags.

The camera crew was already positioned by the front door by the time I got there. The boom operator stood behind me, holding a long microphone right above me but away from the camera's view. I took a deep breath and waited for the assistant producer to call action before opening the door.

I swung the front door open eagerly. My eyes bulged in shock as I took in the sight before me. It wasn't Pierre. This *had* to be a dream.

"What the fuck are you doin' here?" I asked Biggz calmly, through clenched teeth.

My heart felt as if it were falling off a skyscraper as I witnessed from over Biggz' shoulder, Pierre's white Porsche Cayenne pulling up behind Biggz' black Maybach.

CHAPTER TWENTY-FOUR
KoKo

"Yo, we need to talk." Biggz demanded angrily.

Still feeling as if this had to be a dream, I said nothing. My eyes and mouth remained wide open as I tried to speak. Behind him, I watched in horror as Pierre exited the Cayenne.

I looked behind me at the boom operator, then at the camera operator, wondering if the producers had set me up.

"Are you gonna let me in or what?" Biggz asked.

Numb, I stepped aside and allowed Biggz to come in, then shut the door behind me.

"You can't stay here! You gotta hide! You gotta hide!" I said frantically, pressing both my palms against his chest, in an attempt to move him.

"I don't give a damn bout these fuckin cameras, shorty. We need to talk."

"Biggz, please. Pierre's outside." I whispered.

The mention of Pierre seemed to rile him up even more. "I don't give a fuck about that corny ass nigga! I said we need to talk!"

I tried pushing against his chest again with all of my might, then stared straight into his eyes as my own filled with tears. "Okay, Okay! We can talk! Just let me get rid of him first. Please, Biggz. Just go hide, please." I whispered, not bothering to hide the desperation in my voice.

I didn't care that the cameras were there. Nor did I care that Pierre would eventually see the footage when he watched the show. I would make sure we made it down the altar before the show aired. I knew Pierre didn't agree with divorce. He had said himself that once we said our I Do's, there was no turning back.

Biggz grabbed both my wrists. "Y'all not gonna keep me away from my baby. I want my seed under my motherfuckin' roof! It's either we're gonna be together, maybe even get married, or I'm filing for sole custody, KoKo. I'll be damned if my jit runnin around callin' another nigga daddy."

"Come again?" I heard Pierre's voice ask from behind me.

I dropped my head in defeat as Biggz's voice boomed. "You heard me, nigga! I ain't lettin' no other nigga raise my seed! You got an issue with that, pretty boy?"

"KoKo?" I could hear the hurt in Pierre's voice as he called out for me.

I turned around, not bothering to wipe the flood of tears breaking through my eyelids. I walked towards Pierre with outstretched arms. "I'm so sorry, baby. Please forgive me."

His handsome chiseled face looked torn and his own eyes were fighting to hold back tears as he pushed my arms away.

Pierre glanced around our vast living room at the production crew, as well as Rachel and Melany, who had both come out to investigate what all the ruckus was about.

KOKO

"I'm sorry we've, excuse me, *she's* wasted everyone's time, including my own, but this wedding is off. Well at least our wedding is. *They* may still want to get married." He announced, pointing his chin in Biggz' direction. "She don't know what to do with a good man when she has one." He looked directly at the camera. "Fellas, listen up. Sometimes it just doesn't pay to be the nice guy. Some women only respect men who treat them like shit!"

I tugged at Pierre's arm. "Baby, please don't do this." I whispered.

His eyes peered into mine and his mouth twisted into a look of disgust "We're *over*." He whispered with a venom I'd never heard from him before.

"Baby, no. What about J'adore?" I whimpered.

Pierre's face was filled with rage. "You have this *thug* in my house claiming that the baby growing inside of you is his!"

"Baby, calm down, please." I urged.

I noticed two uniformed security personnel on standby just a few feet from us. Again, I couldn't help wondering if this had been a setup. Unfortunately, Pierre was unfazed with the presence of the built security guards nearby. Being a professional fitness trainer, Pierre was no small dude himself. Biggz would also be a challenge for them to hold back since he was both tall and wide in stature.

Biggz spoke up behind me. "Look KoKo, that offer I gave you awhile back still stands, baby. Just move in with me, you wont have to work another day of your life. You don't need this corny ass nigga."

Now why the fuck did he have to go and say that shit?

I caught a look of curiosity from Pierre. "So exactly how long have you two been sleeping around?" Pierre asked Biggz.

"Don't say *shit* to me, nigga." Biggz spat.

Pierre took a step around me and gave Biggz a death stare.

I grabbed his arm. "B-baby, please-" I stammered.

He ignored me and pointed a finger at him. "Oh, you can't talk man to man? I wanna know how long you been fuckin my girl?!" Pierre asked with so much vigor, his long dreds shook.

"Look, you corny motherfucka, you don't know your girl as well as I do. I know the real KoKo. I know what she likes. It ain't my fault she fell in love with this dick!" Biggz said, grabbing the front of his pants with an air of arrogance as he continued, "She said you weren't big enough to lay it down properly at home, so she wanted me to show her how a *real* nigga lay down pipe, bitch."

I quickly interjected. "Now hold on a damn minute, Biggz. I never said that!" My curls swung as I quickly looked from Biggz to Pierre and back to Biggz. "I said the sex was boring. I never said nothing about the size of my man's dick."

"The sex is boring?" I heard Pierre repeat behind me.

Biggz snickered.

I turned to face Pierre once again. "Baby, that's not what I meant. Why don't we talk about this later without the cameras? Please." I whispered.

His locs swayed from side to side as he shook his head. "So, I bore you in bed, hunh? That's why you're running around spreading your legs for everyone? Is J'adore even mine?"

I gasped. "Of course, J'adore is yours, Pierre! Who else's would she be?!" I shouted in anger.

The corner of his top lip curled as he stared at me. "It all makes sense now. All of a sudden you wanting to stick your tongue in my ass?"

My face grew hot with humiliation. "What are you talkin' about, Pierre?" I asked. I was praying inside that he could read the desperate pleas in my eyes for him to not expose me like this. At least not while the cameras were rolling.

Behind me, Biggz began to guffaw as if he'd just heard the funniest thing in the world.

"What the fuck is so funny?" Pierre snapped.

Biggz held up both his hands in front of his chest in surrender. "Nothin man, don't mind me. Just thought shit was funny. I told her not to try that shit on your square ass. But lemme ask you this: you ever try it on her? Man," He started as he lit up a cigar. "That shit drives her *wild*. That bitch is a straight freak. We got ourselves a winner right there."

"Fuck you, you fat muthafucka!' I spat.

Biggz chuckled. "Fat muthafucka, hunh? The same fat muthafucka who taught you how to lick a nigga's ass, hunh? Then go home to kiss ya boy with that same mouth, you nasty, bitch."

I was stunned. Before I knew it or could stop him, I was pushed to the side by Pierre as he bum-rushed Biggz. Luckily the two security guards had anticipated it and quickly pulled the two apart.

"Let go of me, I'm cool." Pierre assured. He glanced at me. "She's not worth it anyway."

I tried to grab his arm, but he pushed me away.

"Pierre, baby, he's lying."

Biggz chuckled. "May God strike me dead if I'm lying."

"You're lying!" I took a step forward.

"So, I never introduced you to that?"

"Hell no! Moet did, *bitch*!" I spat.

"She did? Right, okay." He said sarcastically.

"*She*?" Pierre asked. "You're gay?"

"I am *not* gay." I said.

"Shittin' me." Biggz guffawed.

Pierre stared at me. "Who are you?"

"Why don't we talk about this alone? I'll explain everything." I suggested.

"I'm done. You can have her." He said to Biggz, then turned to leave.

"Pierre, wait!" I cried out behind him.

"Don't fuckin' say my name! This is exactly why I was against this reality show bullshit!" He shouted as he stormed out the front door.

I followed behind him. "Pierre! Let's talk about this privately." I pleaded.

He opened the passenger side door of his Cayenne and hopped in. I stopped dead in my tracks when I peeped a familiar light-skinned chick in the driver's seat of his car. The car I had purchased a year ago as a gift for Pierre. Feelings of anger, confusion, and hurt suddenly filled me. What was she doing outside our house in the driver's seat of his car?

Pierre rolled down the window. "I'll be here to get J'adore when they leave."

KOKO

I cocked my head to the side to get a better look at the bitch. "Who are you?" I asked, ignoring Pierre.

Pierre turned to face the singer. "Please just ignore her. She know exactly who the fuck you are."

Armani shielded her face with her hand. "Please no cameras! I do not authorize being filmed." She shouted at the crew behind me.

"You fuckin this bitch?" I asked Pierre.

Armani snickered. I cocked my head again to make eye contact with the whore. "Amusing, ain't it?"

"Look, this is between the two of you. We were about to start my fitness training when he received a call from your producers. I didn't want him driving all the way here while he was so upset, that's all." She tried explaining. Unfortunately, I wasn't buying it nor did I give a fuck.

"Armani, you don't have to explain yourself to her. Like you said, this is between her and I." Pierre said.

I cut my eyes at her. "Don't you ever bring your ass on my property again. You hear me? *Ever!*"

"She's my client." Pierre reiterated. He looked over at Armani. "Come on, let's get out of here. I'm not entertaining this bullshit."

"Oh wait, before you leave. I have something for you." I said.

I quickly jogged over to where a few small black decorative bricks surrounding a few of our plants outside were.

I grabbed two bricks and ran back towards the Porsche.

Running up to the hood of the Porsche, I shouted, "Don't come back with this bitch!"

I threw the bricks one after the other towards the windshield. Both bricks bounced off the windshield but not before leaving small cracks right in front of the driver's side. They then fell on the hood of the luxury vehicle and slid down, leaving a train of black scratches on the white paint as it did so. I bent down and grabbed the fallen bricks.

"Go! Go! Go!" Pierre shouted at Armani as she sped in reverse like a madwoman.

I threw the bricks again but this time they both missed.

The tires screeched and burned rubber as the vehicle flew down the long drive way and past the wrought iron gates.

CHAPTER TWENTY-FIVE
Desi

Ivonka never showed up to see me at the hospital the four days I had been admitted. Each time I tried to call her, I was sent straight to voicemail. It was so unlike her. It wasn't until her boyfriend had Isaac contact me about her whereabouts did I start to panic.

According to Adrian, Ivonka had never came home the night my mother had called her from the the hospital to get the boys. In fact, she had been gone two *whole* days. On the third morning, he called Isaac for my number to see if maybe Ivonne had slept over my house. Isaac informed him that he didn't have a number for me, but would try reaching me at the hospital. Sure enough, Isaac was able to reach me at Mount Sinai. I suggested he try calling every hospital and jail in Miami before calling the cops. In the meantime, I would call my mom and KoKo to see if they'd heard from her. They both had not.

On the day that I was scheduled to be discharged, Isaac called me back to inform me that Ivonka had been involved in a terrible head-on collision that night and had been airlifted to Jackson Memorial Hospital. As much as I missed my kids and wanted to spend time with them, I called an Uber to pick me up the following morning after being released from the jail that I had been transported to after being discharged. I called an Uber to take me to where my friend was and I was not prepared for the news I received once I arrived.

"You Desiree?" A short but handsome stocky black man, with long locs asked, as he spotted me making my way towards the waiting area of the ICU.

"Yeah, that's me."

He nodded. "I'm Isaac. I've heard so much about you."

"How is she?" I immediately asked. I wasn't particularly in the mood for small talk.

"She's been in a coma since she got here."

I shook my head. "That can't be true."

Adamant that Isaac was mistaken, I pushed past him to the nurse's station. One of the nurses confirmed what Isaac told me and said I would have to wait on the physician for more details.

"Can I see her?" I asked the nurse.

She pointed behind me. "You'll have to wait with the family until one of the nurses says it's okay."

"The family?" I asked.

I turned around to find Isaac behind me. "Come on, I'll introduce you to everyone."

We walked over to where an older Hispanic-looking man as well as an older black woman were seated. The man's arm was around the woman as he attempted to console her. She had the same high yellow complexion, high cheekbones, emerald eyes, and what some would call *good hair* as Ivonne. I couldn't help but notice she was wearing white gloves that came up to her elbows. She was impeccably outfitted in what I recognized as a grey knit Chanel pencil-skirt, white blouse, and a large black floppy wool fedora.

"Don't touch me!" The woman chastised the man sharply.

They both looked up as Isaac and I approached them.

"Ms. Roux, this is Desiree, a friend of Ivonka's. Desiree, Ivonka's mother, Collette Roux." Isaac said.

"It's nice to meet you, Ms. Roux." I said to the woman.

She glared at me. "Is it really? Aren't you the one she was on her way to see that night?"

The man besides her nodded. "That's the one."

Isaac continued. "The asshole sitting beside her is Adrian."

Adrian stood up. "Who are you calling an asshole, little man? Don't you have some shelves to stock?"

"Sit down." Ms. Roux instructed Adrian, to which he obliged. She pointed a gloved finger at Isaac. "And you, watch your mouth! I know Rosie and I know she did *not* raise you to use language like that. Especially in front of your elders! I oughta have you scrub that mouth of yours., young man."

"My apologies, ma'am." Isaac said humbly.

Ms. Roux brought her attention back to Adrian. "So you and my daughter been shacking up, hunh?"

Adrian nodded uncomfortably as Isaac snickered.

"How long have you two been dating?" She asked.

"About six months now, I believe." He replied.

She continued. "And what is it that you do?" She asked Adrian.

Adrian frowned "Excuse me?"

"Yes, what is it that you do, son? What kinda work do you do?" She answered impatiently.

"Uh, I'm an engineer, ma'am." Adrian answered.

"Oh? What kind of an engineer?" She asked.

Adrian looked uneasily at me, Isaac, then back to Ms. Roux. "I-uh- a chemical engineer."

Isaac spoke up. "That's funny. Ivonne told me you were a chemist."

Adrian cleared his throat. "She always get the two mixed up. I've been a chemical engineer for the last fourteen years."

"What school did you earn your degree?" Ms. Roux asked sharply.

"University of Illinois." He answered.

"Who's your current employer?" Ms. Roux quickly held up her hand. "You know what, don't answer that. I *will* find out on my own because you see, someone needs to be looking out for Ivonka." She cut her emerald eyes at Isaac in disappointment. "My daughter has a habit of wearing her heart on her sleeve. I blame it on her lack of a father growing up. I'm sure she told you her father died of an aneurysm when she was just ten. Ever since then, she's been in search of that fatherly love in all the wrong places. Often times, scumbags prey on that. Now, I'm not calling you a scumbag, son, at least not until you show your ass."

Adrian nodded. "I understand, Ms. Roux. Please believe, your daughter is in good hands."

"Good, because I'll do everything in my power to bring Ivonka back home to Louisiana with me if I find out otherwise, you hear me?"

This time Isaac spoke up. "Ms. Roux, there's no need-"

Ms, Roux quickly cut him off. "Look Isaac, no offense son, but I don't need Ivonka sharing the same fate as your dear mother. I'll be damn if I let another man mooch off of my daughter. Over my dead body! Do you have any idea how much she's worth?" She asked Adrian sharply.

"Ms. Roux?" I breathed a sigh of relief as a stout black man in a physician's coat approached us.

We all stood.

"Dr. Moore, how's my daughter doing?" Ms. Roux asked.

"Is she gonna make it?" Isaac queried.

"Her heart rate and blood pressure has stabilized. She's lucky to even be alive after a head on collision." He answered.

"Do you think there's a good chance that she'll wake up?" Adrian asked.

Dr. Moore eyed us all as he answered solemnly. "I can't say. Unfortunately, this is one of those conditions that we just can't predict. It could take years, months, or a few days."

Ms. Roux broke down. "Well what am I supposed to do?" She cried as Isaac held her. My heart felt for her as my own eyes welled up with tears.

"Can we see her?" I asked.

Dr. Moore nodded.

Isaac extended a hand to the doctor. "Thank you, doctor." The two men shook hands and Dr. Moore nodded before leaving us to ourselves.

Ms. Roux sniffed. "I need a few moments alone with my daughter." She said before walking off.

Adrian immediately turned to Isaac. "Look little man, I don't know what it is that you been telling that woman, but you need to mind your own business before you get what's coming to you, you hear me?"

Isaac took a step towards Adrian. "Or what?"

I quickly jumped in between them, "Hey! Guys! Is this what you think Ivonne would want? I don't. Now both of you sit the fuck down."

Neither moved.

"*Right now* or I'm calling security." I threatened and both men finally took a seat.

After about twenty minutes, I was finally able to see Ivonne alone. It took everything in me not to break down when I saw her unconscious body laying on that hospital bed hooked up to all different type of machines. Her lean athletic body was covered in a hospital gown and I was surprise to see her short bob replaced with long dark extensions.

This is all my fault, I thought to myself as I slowly approached her.

My lips quivered as I gently touched her hand.

"I'm so sorry, Ivonka." I whispered. This time I didn't try holding back my tears.

"I'm so sorry for being so selfish. I'm so sorry for..for..for *everything!*" I sobbed.

I stared at my beautiful friend. I missed her so much. I would of done anything for her to open her eyes. For me to see her beautiful green eyes and hear that Baton Rouge accent she always trying to disguise. I missed my friend so much. Even unconscious, she was still beautiful. Even if she could never quite see her true beauty in herself.

KOKO

I sniffled then continued. "I filed for divorce as soon as I was discharged. I know what you're thinking. Why would I allow myself to become a statistic: single mother of six. Well, when you think about it, we're all a negative statistic in one way or another. I think my happiness and sanity is more important for me and my children. Dr. Humphrey, the therapist I'm seeing, says my role in Delilah's life will play a big part of the woman she becomes. I don't want my children to think this type of behavior and relationship is okay. I want Delilah to learn to be self-sufficient and to have a good head on her shoulders. I want my sons to know what being a real man is. Although I feel old as fuck, I'm barely in my mid-twenties. Dr. Humphrey says I still have a whole life ahead of me to turn my life around if I wish. And guess what, Vonne? I want to. All I want is to be happy. I've already registered for the next semester at Miami-Dade College. I plan on going full-time as soon as this court shit is over. Guess I should mention that I turned myself in yesterday morning and was released on bond the same day. Lucas says he can convince his little *puta* to drop the charges. We'll see, right? I'm still moving out. I've spoken to my mom and she's agreed to move in with me when I find a house, to help with the boys. My lawyer says he can make sure I get my alimony and child support. That will definitely help pay for a babysitter, housekeeper, and maybe even a nanny while I go to school full-time. I figure I can finally get my nursing degree within a year's time. Wanna know something Ivonne? I should've told you that being married isn't always what its cracked up to be.

Take your time, heal, and fall in love with yourself first before you put yourself out there."

I bent down to give her a gentle kiss on the cheek then turned to leave.

I halted and turned towards the bed. "Oh, one more thing. I finally got to meet Adrian. He is one attractive guy. Finally met Isaac, too. I can tell he loves you a lot. He seems like a genuine friend. I think I prefer Isaac for you. We love you, babe and we need you." I said.

I made my way back to the waiting area to Ms. Roux, Adrian. and Isaac.

"I have to go pick up my children. Can you please keep me updated? I don't care what time it is. Call me anytime. I'll be back tomorrow to see her again." I said to them.

Isaac nodded. "I'll definitely keep you updated."

I looked at Ms. Roux. "Ma'am if there's anything I can do, please don't hesitate to reach out to me."

Ms. Roux did not respond, and instead looked straight ahead. I couldn't blame her. She blamed me for her daughter's coma and so did I.

Isaac spoke up again. "Thanks, Desiree."

I was about to head towards the elevators when I suddenly remembered something.

"Did anyone call Koreen?"

CHAPTER TWENTY-SIX
KoKo

I hadn't gotten out of bed the last two days except to piss and shit. I no longer felt like I had a reason to. J'adore was away with Pierre for the weekend and I refused to continue filming for *A Dream's Wedding*. I mean, what was the fuckin' point? Pierre had called off our engagement and had officially moved out the day he had shown up with that light-skinned bitch, Armani Rayne. I was still unsure if they were dating like the tabloids were suggesting. However, if I found out that they were seeing each other, that bitch would have what's coming to her. I didn't give a fuck how famous she was. Fuck her!

If all of that wasn't bad enough, I lost my endorsement with Melanin Cosmetics. They claimed my recent scandals "wasn't a good look" for their brand. Since severing all ties with Ivonka, I no longer had a trusted attorney to consult with about my business dealings. As a matter of fact, I hadn't heard from Ivonne since our last argument two weeks ago.

"Ms. Wilson?" I opened one eye to see Rachel's head poking in my bedroom door.

"What do you want?" I replied groggily.

"You have a visitor."

I closed my eyes. "Who is it? I'm not getting up to get dressed. Tell them to come back later." I groaned.

"KoKo, it's me and I don't mind seeing you just the way you are. I used to wake up to that face and awful morning breath every morning, remember?" The familiar voice interrupted.

I hastily sat up as both my eyes and mouth fluttered open in disbelief.

"What the hell are you doing here, Bernie?"

My gaze reverted from my ex-husband to my 19-year-old assistant.

"I tried to stop him, Miss Wilson." She began explaining.

I held up a hand. "It's okay, Rachel. You can leave for the day."

She looked alarmed. "Did I-?"

"Relax, you did nothing wrong. You'll still be gettin' paid for the whole day. Just leave before I change my mind, please."

"Thank you, Ms. Wilson." Rachel smiled.

Bernard walked in and shut the door behind him before making his way to my bed. He seemed to never age. His low 'fro was always neatly cropped and he was impeccably dressed head to toe in Ralph Lauren.

"Bernard, I thought I told you what happened was a mistake."

He sat down on the bed besides me. "Yeah, I know and I feel you on that. Trust me."

"Then why are you here, Bernard?" I asked with a hint of annoyance.

"You ain't been answering my calls-"

I quickly cut him off. "I ain't been answering no one's calls." I revealed.

"Look, I know you and dude split up. I just wanted to check on you to make sure you were okay. Last time you were depressed, you stayed in bed and gained a ton of weight, remember?"

I squinted at him in suspicion. "Since when have you ever cared enough to check up on me? If I remember correctly, I didn't get a call, text, or visit from you after I caught you fucking Gary." I snapped.

Bernard's head fell at the mention of my cousin's name. "I wanted to call and I wanted to see you after that whole shit. Your pops brought some goons to my studio and threatened to put a bullet through my fuckin dome if either me or Gary contacted you."

I scrunched my forehead. "My pops said that?"

"Yes."

"How is Gary, anyway? Does he know you're here?" I asked.

Bernard nodded. "He knows."

I rolled my eyes. "Figures. Does he know that the baby might be yours? That you cheated on him with *me*? Never in a million years thought I'd ever be asking that shit." I shook my head at the irony.

Bernie nodded as his eyes gazed away from mine and towards the comforter. Perhaps in shame?

"You know, we got a lot in common. You and I." He said.

I shook my head in disagreement. "We used to. Not anymore we don't."

"We're both bisexual. Both cheated on our significant other-" He started.

I stopped him before he could continue. "Do you really wanna go there, Bernie? I don't think you really wanna go there. What you did- the way you hurt me, was a thousand times worse than what I did." I rebutted.

He furrowed his brows. "In the words of Kanye: '*How Sway*'?"

"Well for one, you and I were *married*. Two, you were caught fucking someone not only related to me but a man on *national* television, Bernie. How is that the same?"

"I think the Koreen from back then and ya fiancé now, have a lot in common, then." He corrected.

"Boy, make up yo mind."

"Your fiancé seem like an upstanding guy. Never heard about him stepping out on you before. You know he was with that choreographer before you-"

"I know. Get to the point." I demanded.

"My point is. I did some background on him years ago."

"For what?" I snapped.

He held up his hands and I allowed him to continue. "All I did was ask around about him. The nigga is squeaky clean. I remember when you were as faithful and loyal to me as he is to you. Now I'm hearing you fucked my boy, Ganja, and some nigga. One of Brick Boss' entourage? What happened to you, Koreen?" He sounded sincere.

"Some nigga? He's a director and a producer. You need to leave, instead of sitting here playing Dr. Phil in my bedroom right now. Pierre could walk in at any minute."

"Look Koreen, I care about you. I've seen you go through all these changes after our divorce. I know that I may be to blame. I mean, what can I say? A nigga fucked up. Seem like you still carrying that shit from the past and it's affecting your future. Let it go. I know I wasn't shit. Shit changed after we both blew up. What I did to you had nothing to do with you, really. Shit just changed. Especially after Ayanna."

A lumped formed in my throat at the mention of our baby girl, Ayanna. This was the first time he had ever mentioned her let alone said her name. Ayanna J'adore Ingram, our baby girl. I was surprise to see that Bernard's eyes were wet.

"You good?" I asked.

He nodded. "I'm good. You know, I want this baby to be mine." He announced, pointing at my belly.

He continued, "Shit, do you know how jealous I was when you and ol' dude had your little girl?' He smiled. "If I could do it all over again, I would've never cheated. I was young. Stupid. I would've loved to try having another baby with you. You were a good woman, Koreen and I wanna apologize for ever hurting you the way I did. I'm sorry."

I stared at him in sympathy. As much as I wanted to continue to hate him for hurting and humiliating me, I couldn't. I still had love for Bernard Ingram. Not that I wanted him back, though. I loved him the same way I loved a relative. My heart belonged to Pierre Woods now. Pierre had never betrayed me. He was a good man to me and didn't deserved to be cheated on and humiliated. I guess Bernard and I were a lot alike in some ways after all.

He sighed then stood up. "Look, I gotta go. I just wanted to check on you since you were in this big ol house by yourself. Oh, I also wanted to give you this." He pulled out a folded white envelope from inside his pants pocket.

"What is it?"

"I had my connection find out who did this to you. Here."

"Well y'all wasted y'all time. I already know who sold me out. That bitch Ivonka." I said, grabbing the envelope.

"Just check it out and thank me later. It was the least I could do." He said as he eyed the pack of Newport Lights on my nightstand.

"I'll take these." He grabbed the pack of cigarettes before turning to leave and I groaned inwardly.

My cigarettes had been the only thing keeping me sane for the past 72 hours.

"Fine, take 'em." I relented. "Hey, Bernie..." I called out to him just as he reached for the knob.

He turned to face me. "Whassup?"

"Thank you for coming to see me, check on me, whatever. I needed this." And I meant every word of it. In some way, I felt like I was finally on my way to having that closure I needed to heal.

After Bernie left, I decided I should finally get up, eat breakfast, shower, and head to the gym. As soon as I grabbed the keys to the Rover, Desi called me.

"Everything okay?" I asked immediately, thinking of her recent suicide attempt.

Desi groaned. "I'm fine. Have you gone to see Ivonne?"

"Hell naw! Fuck her! Why in the fuck would I go see her?" I snapped.

She took in a deep breath. "Ivonka's in the hospital, KoKo."

"So?" I shrugged as if she could see me over the phone. "I don't give a fuck. Fuck that bitch. That's karma for her ass. Praise God! *Won't He do it?*" I gloated.

"Koreen-" Desi started.

I quickly interjected. "Don't ask me to go see that bitch either, Desi. What happened? Ms. Bourgie Barbie done broke a leg or somethin'?"

"If you would shut up and let me talk!" Desi huffed.

"Talk then, heiffa, I'm listenin'." I snapped back.

"Ivonka's in a coma. They don't know if she'll ever wake up-"

"Hunh? *A coma?*" I asked. My heart seemed to be racing and falling at the same time. The room was spinning as I crouched to my knees and kept my eyes on the ground. What the fuck was going on? The last two weeks felt like I was living in the Twilight Zone.

Desiree was still on the other end talking. "Hello? Did you hear me? Koreen! KoKo! *Hellooooo?*"

"Hunh?"

"I said do you want me to come with you to see her? My mom still got the kids. I can be at your place in less than ten minutes." I couldn't tell if she was asking or telling me. I was too distracted by the deep sense of dread overtaking me.

"Get dressed. I'm already on my way." She instructed before ending the call.

It wasn't until she hung up did I think to ask what had happened.

***

"Well that was fast. I thought I'd be waitin' a good hour for you to get ready. You know how you do. Those sneakers are hot, too." Desiree said as soon as I'd gotten inside the German minivan.

"I was on my way to the gym when you called." I said, feeling numb.

"The gym? Girl you've lost weight since we last seen each other. Don't stress too much. Not good for the baby." She said, pulling away from my driveway.

"What happened to Ivonne?" I could barely say her name without my throat feeling tight and my eyes tearing up. It had to be the hormones.

"Head on collision with a party bus." She answered.

"When?"

Her voice wavered as she spoke. "The night I overdosed. She was on her way to pick up the boys." Desi replied. "And yes, it's my fault and I do feel guilty, but there's nothing I can do about it now but be there for her and her family. If it weren't for Dr. Humphrey, I'd probably have tried overdosing again after seeing Ivonne in that hospital."

I didn't know who the fuck Dr. Humphrey was nor did I care.

"It's my fault." I whispered.

Desiree quickly glanced at me, then lowered the volume of the radio. "You say somethin?"

"I did this." I said a little louder. "We got in a big ass argument. Right before we hung up that night, I told her I wouldn't care if both of you died that night." I dabbed my eyes with the sleeve of my t-shirt.

"You said that?"

"I didn't mean it. I was upset. Obviously, I didn't mean it. I even came to see you at the hospital the next day. I was just talkin' shit."

Desi remained silent as the muscles in her face hardened.

Remembering that I had brought along the envelope that Bernie had given me, I pulled it out of my Chanel handbag and began to read the information as Desi drove over the MacArthur Causeway in silence.

CHAPTER TWENTY-SEVEN
KoKo

By the time we reached the 6th floor of Jackson Memorial Hospital, I was drowning in a flood of emotions. So much so, that as soon as I laid eyes on Adrian's bitch-ass standing against the wall of the lobby, I thought of my last conversation with him and Ivonne.

My 5-foot-7 frame immediately lunged for his tall muscular build.

"You muthafucka! I hate you! I hate you!" I shouted at him through tears as I began pounding away at his face.

Adrian grabbed both my wrists. "Yo, somebody better come get this bitch!"

Without thinking, I used my knee to kick him in the groin. Adrian released his grip on me and went crashing to the ground. Just as quick as he had fallen to the ground holding his nuts, he began connecting powerful blows to my ankle with his fist, resulting in me toppling over and landing painfully on my back and tailbone.

"*Dios mio!* She's pregnant! She's pregnant!" I heard Desiree shouting in the distance.

Everything seemed to be moving so fast as I rolled over to my knees to lung on top of that motherfucker again. Fortunately for Adrian, someone was holding me back.

"*It was him!*" I cried, not giving a damn that snot was running all over my face. "*You came between us, motherfucker! You're a piece of shit!*"

"This bitch is crazy! Why is she here??" Adrian shouted as he tried his best to stand to his feet. Isaac quickly made his way between us, although I was still being restrained by Desi and now another woman.

"This motherfucka," I pointed at the loser. "Set me up this whole time. Recorded my telephone conversations and sold it to the tabloids. I got proof! He's nothing but a fucking user! You don't even have a fucking job!"

"That's a lie! Someone need to escort this bitch outta here!" He shouted as an older woman wearing a large fedora and long white gloves made her way to the small crowd that was forming.

"I know who the fuck you really are!"

Adrian chuckled uncomfortably and shook his head.

"Yeah, I know all about you, fuck-nigga!" I snarled.

"Did you find out who your baby daddy is, too?"

I lunged at him and grew even more angry when Desi and a young woman pushed me back. "Get the fuck offa me!" I shouted at them.

"KoKo, relax!" Desi shouted.

A trail of nurses and other hospital personnel made their way to the crowd. "Please everyone turn your phones off!" A nurse instructed the bystanders who were recording the debacle.

"I gotta ask one of you to leave or you both will have to go." A security guard's voice boomed.

"Escort her out!" Adrian shouted as he pointed a paw at me. "My fiancé is in a coma on life support right now! This bitch wasn't even her friend!"

The woman holding me back gasped.

"Ms. Wilson," The heavy-set guard started softly, "I'd hate to have to escort you out in front of all these people. If could just cooperate and leave…"

"Absolutely *not*." The high-yellow woman with the long gloves interrupted in what sounded like a New Orleans accent. "I need you to escort *this* man out." She pointed to Adrian, who's face was now covered with a look of sheer disbelief. "We're family. He's not."

CHAPTER TWENTY-EIGHT
KoKo

Every bad seed of emotion, every grudge, every feeling of hatred, every negative emotion towards Ivonka Nicolette Roux dissipated when I laid eyes on her.

"*Vonne, wake up.*" I was sobbing into her bosom as Isaac and Desiree tried to pull me away.

"KoKo," Isaac whispered sharply behind me. "You need to calm down, or they're gonna ask you to leave."

"Koreen, calm down, baby girl." Desi consoled me, rubbing my back.

I lowered my sobs to a mumble as tears rolled down the bridge of my nose and onto Ivonka's hospital gown.

"*I didn't mean it. I didn't mean, Vonne. Come back. I didn't mean it.*" I repeated, hoping that it would somehow bring my best friend back.

Instead of her eyes fluttering open to reveal her beautiful bright green eyes, she remained still with the sounds of the heart monitor beeping in a rhythm beside us.

Desi's pulled at my arm "Koreen, we'll come back after you've calmed down a bit." She tried convincing me.

This time I didn't hold back my guttural wails as my muscles weakened and I crumpled to the ground

"*Wake up! I'm sooooorry, Voooonne! I'm sorryyyy! I didn't mean it! Pleeeease, Voooonne. I didn't mean it! Oh, god!*"

Isaac tried lifting me as Desi held on to my arm.

"Stop it, Koreen. This is not what Ivonka would've wanted!" Desi whispered sharply.

"What in the world is going on here?" Ms. Roux asked as she busted in with two nurses.

My wails decreased to low moans as sharp pains attacked my abdomen. Isaac lifted me into his arms as I wrapped my arm around my stomach.

"Ma'am, sir. We're gonna have to ask you to leave the room." One of the nurses instructed as the other nurse checked the machines.

Ms. Roux's Jimmy Choo's clicked against the hospital floor as she angrily made her way to me.

"Now listen clearly, young lady. My daughter is *not* dead. You hear me? She is *not* dead. I won't stand for anyone hootin' and hollerin' as long as my daughter has breath in her. You hear me?" She chastised. *"Do you hear me?"*

I nodded slowly as I tried to stop a wave of fresh tears from forming.

Behind me Desi released a gasp. "Oh my god, she's bleeding! She's bleeding!" She cried out as my pink leggings began to feel as if I'd just wet myself.

CHAPTER TWENTY-NINE
Ivonne

"You've always the meant the world to me, Ivonka Roux. Even if you've always overlooked me. I fell for you the moment we locked eyes at Mozelle's party. Remember that? Shit, I think even back then that chump, Francois Lewis, could feel the chemistry between us. Don't you agree?

Do you know how hard it is to have to hear you talk about all these losers you've been with? It's been hard, Ivonne. I've always wanted the best for you. Even if it's with someone else."

"Hey Vonne, it me, Desiree. We're all still praying for you to pull through, baby girl. You got this! Besides, Delilah needs her auntie. Anyway, te amo, mi amiga."

"Ivonne, I don't know what's going on. Why won't you wake up? It's been 4 months now and you're still......asleep. Jada wanted me to tell you she misses you. She still doesn't quite understand that you're here but not here. Before you start worrying, my baby is okay. I'm still pregnant. I was placed on bedrest for a short time, though. My mom moved in with me temporarily and everything during that time. Girl, it was awful. By the way, I was able get out of my contract with the reality show, thanks to the amended contract you drew up. I love you, Ivonka Roux. I wish you'd wake up, doll."

"Hey beautiful, it's me again. Guess what? I was able to land a better job at a warehouse. I been thinking about *maybe driving big rigs. Heard there's a lot of money to be made in the trucking business. Of course, I'd have to get my trucking license. I plan on working at the warehouse overnight and attend trucking classes during the day. Might as well just travel cross-country. Not like I have anything back home. No wife or kid, right."* Isaac chuckled.

"Go for it." I mumbled.

I squinted as my eyes tried adjusting to the awfully bright lights.

"Nurse! Nurse!"

There was suddenly a heap of commotion surrounding me. I tried sitting up but was gently pushed down by a white woman in a nurse's uniform.

What in the world?

"Ms. Roux, we're gonna need you to lay still. Don't get up, alright?"

"Can you tell us your name?" A man dressed in plain clothing asked.

"Ivonka."

"Can you tell us your birthday?" He asked.

"March sixteenth. Seventeenth?" I responded with uncertainty, feeling as if this were a test question.

"My god! My baby!" I was shocked to see my mother running towards me.

"Ma'am! Please, wait in the lobby! Ma'am! Somebody get here!" The man shouted.

"Mommy?" I whispered.

What on God's green earth was my mother doing in my bedroom? What were all these people doing in here? Where was Adrian?

KOKO

That's when I remembered jumping in one of my vehicles. The white Bentley, I believe. I remembered leaving my compound in a rush to meet someone at the hospital. Someone had called me with a sense of urgency. I want to say Desiree. No, Desiree had been the one in the hospital. Nevertheless, I was rushing when I received a call on my cell from Adrian.

"Look babe. There's something I need to tell you." I heard him say through the car speakers.

"Can it wait 'til I get home? I need to call Koreen to let her know about Desi-"

Adrian interrupted. "This is about KoKo. I feel like you need to know that I tapped your phone. I feel like someone needed to expose that bitch once and for all."

For a split second he sounded like he was speaking a foreign language. He had to be.

"Wait, what are you talking about, Adrian? You tapped my line? You promised me you'd keep everything-"

"Look, it's nothing personal against you but I thought you should know since I won't be here when you get back. The truth is, I was never a chemist. I've been working as a barber on and off for the last fifteen years. I'm also married."

"You're married?"

"Me and Val are separated but we're still technically married. I was snooping through her phone a couple months back when I found picture messages from KoKo. Seen text messages of her referring to my wife as *Moet*. I found out about the threesomes they were regularly having. I had to get to KoKo somehow. She had to pay. I had to expose her for the homewrecking thot that she is. I sold the stories to the tabloids. I'm sorry it had to be through you. It's nothing personal, Ivonka. You're a great woman but I'm in love with my wife."

No, no, no, not again! A feeling of sorrow filled me at the realization that Adrian, the man I had believed was my prince charming, my king, was just another name among the long list of men who had disappointed me. Men who I had given my all to. Men who I had sacrificed everything for. I just couldn't understand why good women like me were always overlooked while women like KoKo had marriage proposals from every direction.

With a heavy heart, my eyes blurred with tears. It wasn't until it was too late that I realized that I had unintentionally crossed over to the other lane. The last image I could remember were two blinding headlights and a fog horn. As I jerked the wheel to get back on the right side of the street, the bright headlights did the same.

"Glad to see you finally up." Isaac greeted with a soft kiss to my forehead.

"I feel like shit." I moaned as I looked around the hospital room. "Where's my mom."

"She went down to the cafeteria to complain about the hospital food."

I laughed. "That sounds about right.

Isaac smiled. "You just don't know how much I've missed that smile. I've missed you so much. We all have."

I thought about how funny it was that Isaac was the first face I had awoken to when I came out of my coma. Lately, every time I took a nap and awakened, his face was always there......waiting.

He seemed to have gone through a transition as well. His face was neatly groomed. His clothes were pressed and had drastically improved. He even walked and carried himself with a little more confidence. I was surprise to find myself *attracted* to Isaac.

I often thought about the last time his lips had pressed against mine and would become aroused. Maybe I had been wrong all along. Maybe, just maybe, Isaac was my prince in shining armor.

"I've been seeing this girl from my old job. She worked in the HR department at Walmart. Her name's Michelle Reese. She's amazing. I think you'd like her. She kinda reminds me of you too, it's funny." He smiled.

I caught myself frowning with disappointment at the revelation.

He held up both hands. "Alright, alright. Maybe not exactly like you. There can only be one Ivonka. I know. Here look at these." He pushed his android onto my hands. "Isn't she stunning?"

I quietly flipped through the pictures as the sounds of Isaac's excited chattering faded to the background.

There was no denying how beautiful the woman was. I could see a resemblance between her and I. We both shared a bright yellow hue and slanted eyes. She kept her mane in a short bob like I had always kept mine before meeting Adrian.

I handed him back his phone. "She's beautiful." I smiled.

He beamed. "Thank you. Oh, before I forget, my mom wanted me to tell you that she wanted to make it to see you, but she's been ill."

"Is she okay?" I asked, concerned.

"Cancer. It came back." He answered solemnly.

"I'm so sorry, Isaac. I have to send her flowers or something."

"Don't." He said. "She says flowers are for the dead and she ain't dead yet." He chuckled.

I was happy to see him laughing again. He planted a kiss on my cheek just as my mom sauntered in.

I desperately wanted to tell him how I'd been wrong and how maybe we should give us a try. The next day I vowed to myself to lay it all out on the table and tell him how wrong I had been. How I was too busy caring about what others would think about me dating him, instead of me giving a good man like *him* a chance.

Unfortunately, that next afternoon, Isaac brought Michelle with him to see me.

She was even more beautiful in person. She had also been the one responsible for Isaac's whole transformation.

"He just needed a lil guidance that was all." She said as she smiled at him.

I knew then by the way he looked at her in response with admiration, that I had lost him.

I had missed my chance. It was already too late.

KOKO

EPILOGUE
Koreen Wilson

Kiana Monroe Wilson was born prematurely on my birthday that same year. I wasn't sure if that was a sign of some sort. We're all still waiting on the DNA test to determine who's the biological father of baby Kiana. I gotta hand it to Pierre for showing up for the birth of my daughter. He was just that kind of guy. An upstanding guy. Biggz had come by to see Kiana a few hours after giving birth. I had asked them both to not take any pictures of the baby. I was planning to sell pictures of Kiana to a reputable magazine but I wasn't telling anyone about that.

Pierre and I ended up selling the 9-bedroom mansion that we shared after it was clear that he had no intentions on coming back home. Pierre had even gone as far as fighting for full custody of J'adore. I think he did it so that I wouldn't put him on child support. He told the judge that he didn't think I was the type of role model that our daughter needed to look up to. Whatever that means. I laughed in his face when the courts granted us shared custody.

As far as my dating life, Moet and I ended up purchasing a townhome together overlooking the beach. We still participated in threesomes from time to time but now there was no need to hide it now that we were together.

I wasn't the only one who had moved within the past year. Desiree's divorce to Lucas would be final in a couple of weeks. As promised, Desiree purchased a home and moved her mom in. Both her mom and the new nanny helped out with the kids while she pursued her nursing degree. In fact, she was expected to graduate next year.

After the whole fiasco with Adrian, Ivonka relocated to Los Angeles to open a second firm. Last I heard, she was still unmarried and single but this time by choice. She claimed she was now taking the time to enjoy what life had to offer. She was a part of a women's traveling club where a group of women travelled all over the world together. She had even taken an interest in acting in local theaters. I couldn't help but to give her the side eye when she mentioned bumping into a famous director at a Hollywood party. She claimed this director had been persistent in courting her even after she continuously turned him down. She said she just wasn't ready to date again. She wanted to heal first and he agreed to wait for her.

Isaac and Michelle were still going strong. He moved back to Baton Rouge to take care of his dying mother and Michelle moved with him. Unfortunately for him, his mother passed shortly after he relocated back home. In her will, she mentioned that she was leaving him a multimillion dollar insurance policy in the hopes of starting a new family legacy.

Isaac and Michelle weren't the only two in love. Pierre and Armani had recently engaged after only knowing each other a couple of months. I bribed J'adore with treats and gifts regularly for information about their wedding. There was no way I was gonna

KOKO

let that fairy tale happen. I was determined to bring my family back together again.

By all means necessary.

TO BE CONTINUED
in
ARMANI
the Hottie

KOKO

If you or anyone else are having suicidal thoughts, please call 9-1-1. You don't have to suffer alone.
SUICIDE PREVENTION HOTLINES

(http://ibpf.org/resource/list-international-suicide-hotlines)

- Argentina: +5402234930430
- Australia: 131114
- Austria: 017133374
- Belgium: 106
- Botswana: 3911270
- Brazil: 212339191
- Canada: 5147234000 (Montreal); 18662773553 (outside Montreal)
- Croatia: 014833888
- Denmark: +4570201201
- Egypt: 7621602
- Finland: 010 195 202
- France: 0145394000
- Germany: 08001810771
- Holland: 09000767
- Hong Kong: +852 2382 0000
- Hungary: 116123
- India: 8888817666
- Ireland: +4408457909090
- Italy: 800860022
- Japan: +810352869090
- Mexico: 5255102550
- New Zealand: 045861048
- Norway: +4781533300
- Philippines: 028969191
- Poland: 5270000
- Russia: 0078202577577
- Spain: 914590050
- South Africa: 0514445691
- Sweden: 46317112400
- Switzerland: 143
- United Kingdom: 08457909090
- USA: 18002738255

ACKNOWLEDGEMENTS

I really didn't want to even write acknowledgements because there are just way too many to thank. So, if I leave anyone out, as the saying goes, *please charge it to my head and not my heart.*

First and foremost, I have to thank the All-Knowing Creator. The same creator that can be found in us all. I have a theory that our existence wasn't a coincidence or by accident. If that were so, how would one explain the varying "gifts" we were all gifted? I also need to thank my mom for passing down the writing gene and my daughter for putting up with my obsession with writing.

Shout out to my day-ones: Brenda Pierre, Marlene Casimir, and Jeremy Dennis. Thank you for always believing in me before I started believing in myself. To my second families: W.B.A.C and The Candy Shop. As well as my other family members: Sepri Stanback and Victoria Boyd. Thank you for supporting my endeavors in more ways than one.

Big special thanks to Jasmine Rivers, of *Advance Magazine*. Thank you for taking the time to look over the beginning stages of my work up until the finished product. You have no idea how much I've appreciated your support.

Last but not least, I'd like to acknowledge and give a special shout out to all bookworms. With the increased usage of technology, reading isn't as popular as it used to be, in my opinion. Thank you to those who still pick up a book and read regularly and from time to time. You're definitely very much appreciated.